TIBETAN SPRING

TIBETAN SPRING

A NOVEL

BY

MARK STEPHEN LEVY

www.whitefalconpublishing.com

TIBETAN SPRING

Mark Stephen Levy

www.whitefalconpublishing.com

First Edition, 2020

ISBN - 978-93-89932-46-1

If you wish to contact the author, his email address is:
markstephenlevy70@gmail.com

Acknowledgement

This story is a love letter to Tibet. Having traveled to Tibet in the 1980's, and spent an enthralling and captivating time there, left a lasting impression of spirituality with the likes I have never experienced. And yet, as time goes on, this sacred spirituality and the city of Lhasa become more and more tempered.

It is my hope that this story and the plea for autonomy becomes a reality, and any Tibetan refugee can return to their homeland.

Wherever you find happiness, that is your home.
- Tibetan proverb

Introduction

After a long cold winter, spring is a joyous time in Tibet. However, in March of 1959, the mood was nothing but somber and anxious for fear that there would be an all-out assault on Lhasa. The Chinese PLA, or People's Liberation Army began their occupation of Tibet in 1950. In the subsequent years, thousands of Tibetans were injured and killed or placed in prison while multiple sacred temples were destroyed. The PLA quickly closed in on Lhasa that March of '59.

Rumors and fear were rampant within various circles in Lhasa that the twenty-three-year-old His Holiness, the Dalai Lama would be taken prisoner or even killed. His Holiness consulted with his advisors and the inner circle of how to handle this impending threat. He had decided to set out for sanctuary in neighboring India.

Under the cover of the night on March 17, the Dalai Lama dressed as a Tibetan soldier, vacated his stately Potala Palace and set out for a grueling journey to India. With an entourage of cabinet members and soldiers, attendants, some family members including his mother, the Dalai Lama successfully escaped out of Lhasa. But the danger was just beginning. To reach the border of India, they would need to pass over several high passes through the Himalayas. All on foot, sometimes horseback, they traveled only by night to avoid Chinese soldiers that could be lurking anywhere.

The grueling journey was disrupted by sickness and exhaustion and always the fear of being discovered by the PLA. Little did the Dalai Lama know, thousands more Tibetans were following in his footsteps. The exodus took about two weeks to arrive at the border of India. It was another one-week march to the Northeast Frontier Indian town of Bomdila where His Holiness received a telegram from India's Prime Minister, Nehru welcoming him to India.

The Dalai Lama was relieved and happy to be in India as Lhasa had become so extreme, filled with pressure, beset with danger. In India, he would be free to practice his sacred Tibetan Buddhism and speak whatever was on his mind with no reprisals from India or anywhere. Ultimately, the Dalai Lama settled in the Himalayan town of Dharmshala, building a temple with various prayer rooms and a large gathering plaza in the middle. He continues to reside there today.

Despite on and off talks and messages through the years with the Chinese government to pave the way for his return, all these efforts proved fruitless. The Dalai Lama remains in India today while traveling the world where throngs of people turn out to hear what this revered religious leader has to say.

Regardless of how happy and settled he is in India, His Holiness' definitive goal remains the same for his people and himself: to return to their homeland of Tibet.

PROLOGUE

TEN YEARS AGO

Visiting Tibet had been Li's dream ever since he understood the plight of the Tibetan people. He felt a huge sadness for them and yet equally intrigued by their mysterious and spiritual culture. Li was the son of a high-ranking member of the group that oversees China, the Central Politburo of the Communist Party. He had recently become a soldier in the PLA and knew exactly where he wanted to be stationed. His father had been just promoted to the second top post, General Secretary, and Li knew his father would be preoccupied with his new duties. Shortly after his army graduation, Li approached his father to tell him he wanted to be stationed in Lhasa.

At first, his father, a stern and serious man, objected to his son's station request. They had a quarrel over it which went on for a week or so. Li was disconsolate and avoided his father. One day, he was summoned to his father's office inside the Politburo. Li sat there stoically in anticipation of a final disappointment, but instead, his father agreed to his transfer to Lhasa. He told his son that he too secretly liked Tibet. He asked his father why he had made such a fuss. He told him that he liked having him close, but it would also be good to leave home for a while. The young soldier was overjoyed and went to his room to apply.

Within days of his fateful meeting with his father, Li took the three-day train ride to Lhasa. Upon arriving, the four-thousand-meter elevation made him feel strange and slow, and his words were slurred a bit. He was told to drink a lot of water with gradual movements to adjust quickly. After resting for two days in his bunker with the other newly minted soldiers, he was assigned to his post in the heart of Tibet, the holy Jokhang Temple.

Li's superior told him it was auspicious to be stationed at the Jokhang and a prestigious assignment. His superior also told him the respected placement was because of his father. Li detected some resentment in his superior's voice, but he promptly dismissed it. Li was happy to observe the fascinating daily rituals of Tibetan culture. He marveled at the Tibetans as they walked round and round in clockwise fashion circling the Jokhang. They would either walk slowly, or prostrate bending parallel to the ground by using wood blocks to slide into fully extended prostrations, stand straight, clap the two blocks together, then walk two steps and prostrate again.

It was a daily ritual of continuously circumambulating around the Jokhang and into the Barkhor Bazaar, a marketplace that surrounded the sanctified temple. People would buy their everyday food and chat amongst themselves of any latest rumors of uprisings and further Chinese intervention eroding their culture. Or simply neighborhood gossip. They would then move on endlessly around the temple once again, repeating on and off throughout the day and evening. Li loved the sounds of quiet chants by the people, all the while twirling their prayer wheels.

In the first few days of his new post, the handsome young Chinese soldier stood silent and emotionless as he was trained to be. But inwardly, he felt such pleasure to be in this holiest and most inspiring of places and looked forward to each day. On his fourth day, he noticed a usually beautiful Tibetan woman who was accompanied by an older woman. *They both look regal*, Li thought. They wore the same Tibetan dress, or *chuba,* a long spacious robe with wide sleeves, and a silver ring decorated with a huge ornament of turquoise in their left ear and long, dark braided ponytails.

Every day now, the soldier would keep a keen eye for this beautiful woman, and every day, he would get a brief rush of excitement when he spotted her. Once they exchanged an innocent glance, but they usually disregarded him. The soldier would often attempt to gain their attention by discreetly yet awkwardly following them with his eyes. This frustrated him but he also realized that in the eyes and minds of Tibetans, he was thought of as the antagonist. Any interaction was prohibited by his superiors unless called for. Many days passed by, and each day brightened when he saw the woman. He assumed the older woman was her mother. Li even worked on his days off just to see her. Still, they never looked his way.

***

It was a warm spring day. The kind of day Tibetans live for through their harsh winters. Li stood at his station. By now, he easily recognized many of the people, yet there were always new faces. Pilgrims would arrive from all over Tibet, spilling into Lhasa, fulfilling their lifelong dream, and join the circumambulation around the Jokhang Temple and into the Barkhor Bazaar.

Li had been at his post for a few hours and had not yet seen the mysterious woman. Li quickly glanced at his watch. When he looked up, they had joined in the ritualistic procession. He broke PLA regulation by displaying a wide smile and a sense of relief. But the relief was temporary. He noticed the elder woman was walking much slower. Unexpectedly, the elder woman fell to the ground. The younger woman tried to grasp her around the waist, but both fell. The soldier didn't hesitate and instinctively ran towards them. He bent to his knees, feeling for a pulse. Anguish was written all over the young woman's face.

Li gave her mouth to mouth resuscitation while alternating massaging her heart. People gathered around in panic. The soldier lifted the woman up and carried her over to a nearby clinic for treatment. Once inside, Li loudly summoned for the doctor, carrying her to an empty room. The younger woman was dutifully by her side. The elder woman started to rattle and shake. The younger woman cried, while the soldier rested his hand on her shoulder with an attempt to comfort her. The shaking had stopped. The younger woman bent over to her chest, quietly sobbing. "Amala," she whispered into her ear. "Goodbye mama." Li silently and helplessly stood by her side.

Finally, she lifted herself off her mother, and gave her a goodbye kiss to the cheek, while holding her stilled hand, then let go. She turned to the soldier and thanked him for assisting. He spoke to her in broken English, humbly accepting her appreciation. The doctor said he would have her mother taken to her house for prayers and visitation of friends and relatives. She told the soldier, after three days, there would be a sky burial, the transmigration of spirits while carrion birds would eat the remains. She also explained to Li that sky burials were a common practice in Tibet due to lack of diggable land. She invited the soldier to come to her house to attend the Lama's *sutras*, ancient scriptures, so that her mom's soul can be released from purgatory.

There were three days of the gathering at her home. Li attended all three days. The room was quiet except for the soft *sutras* reading. The soldier stood at the back of the main room of the small house, his eyes often fixed on the young Tibetan woman who grieved silently with occasional weeps and sniffs. Once he walked towards her and offered a tissue. Her eyes said thank you as he moved to the back of the room again.

For whatever reason, the soldier was infatuated with this Tibetan woman. Surely, he thought she was beautiful. But there was some inner feeling he couldn't reconcile in his mind other than he just felt something. Something. *What was it?* he wondered. Li also felt tremendous sympathy and compassion for the loss of her mother. For now, he would just flow with the passage of ascension of her mom's soul into heaven. Yet, he was somewhat impatient to know her better. He smiled at the irony realizing he didn't even know her name.

Since the solider was Han Chinese, he was not able to attend the sky burial. Li went back to his post at the Jokhang Temple. He would constantly be on the lookout for the Tibetan woman, and for days she had not made an appearance. He felt sad for her and felt his own sadness and loneliness; alienation was all-consuming being a Chinese soldier in Tibet. Mainly, he missed her presence and felt his feelings for her grow.

***

A week after the passing of her mother, he spotted her lifeless face, as she futilely circumambulated around the Jokhang. In the third circulation, she broke from the flow and approached the soldier. His attention was turned the opposite direction as she advanced towards him, catching him off guard. She thanked him and gave him a blessing for assisting her during the collapse of her mother. He finally asked the young woman her name. "Tenzin." He asked if her name had a meaning. She said her name means the keeper of teachings and protector of Dharma. He told her his name was Li and explained that his name meant strong and powerful. "It is a good combination of meanings," Tenzin said. Interpreting what she said as a positive sign, he summoned up all his courage and asked her if he could offer her tea at a tea stall some time. She agreed to it, and then moved back into circulation. The Chinese soldier was beaming.

Part One

CHAPTER ONE

PRESENT DAY

YANGCHEN WAS WALKING HER dog Lucy when the monsoon season announced its arrival with a deafening clap of thunder. She looked up and saw the darkening clouds overhead knowing rain would soon follow.

"Oh my God," Yangchen blared. "Come on Lucy, let's run."

She lived in a modest home with her parents and siblings in a Tibetan refugee village about ten kilometers from Pokhara, Nepal. At eight years old, Yangchen was already a born trailblazer. She would always lead her brothers and sister on hikes around the village, reciting the Tibetan customary greeting, *Tashi Delek,* to the neighbors. Often, the neighbors would comment amongst one another how nice and polite those kids were.

Yangchen molded herself after Joan of Arc, the eighteen-year-old French girl born leader and heroine that helped alter the course of French history in the 1400's. Her grandfather gave her a children's book version of this story, and Yangchen was fascinated by it. Reading that Joan of Arc was put on trial for various charges by the English and found guilty and burned at the stake, horrified Yangchen. She was most inspired by Joan of Arc's courage.

"I will be a leader just like Joan of Arc," she boldly told her grandfather. "Except, I will not be burned." It was as if Yangchen had formed her life's mission from this story. She loved her grandfather, and even though Yangchen had three siblings, he would privately tell her she was his favorite. It was their secret. He would often tell her of when he and his wife, and Yangchen's father lived in Tibet and what life was like in Lhasa.

"When you are in Lhasa, in the early morning, listen for the monks' chants at Drepung and Sera monasteries. The beautiful sound will stay with you for all of your day."

"It sounds wonderful, Grandfather," Yangchen dreamily said. "I really want to go."

"We cannot, my dear Yangchen," her grandfather responded.

"But why not?"

"Politics and policies, my dear Granddaughter."

Even though Yangchen and her siblings were Nepalese born and raised, she remained proud and fascinated by her Tibetan ethnicity and roots. She put away her Joan of Arc book and started reading all about Tibet, of its proud yet disturbing history. And just like Joan of Arc's France, Tibet had suffered similar fates. This was not lost in the young and impressionable Yangchen, and these concepts were never far from her mind.

As she grew older, her grandfather would tell her further stories about Tibet. The more she heard, the more she wanted to go. He told her that he was a High Lama and would often meet with other leaders and even the Dalai Lama himself. She was enthralled and impressed. He showed her pictures of Lhasa, of the stately Potala Palace and the sacred Jokhang Temple.

"They are beautiful," she exclaimed excitedly. "Do you think I can go one day, Grandfather?"

"I surely hope so, Granddaughter Yangchen." He responded with resignation in his voice.

***

For Yangchen's eighteenth birthday that also coincided with high school graduation, she was given a shiny new smartphone, equipped with all the communication tools one comes to expect from the device. She immediately opened accounts on all the social media platforms. She was the last person in her class to have a phone and friended and followed everyone.

She was overjoyed. Yangchen spent all her free time on her phone chatting with her friends, while combing through news feeds. She even joined Tibet refugee clubs and chatrooms. It was there she made a surprising discovery: almost everyone was like her. The people in these online clubs were classified as Tibetan refugees who came from Nepal, Bhutan, Sikkim and Dharmshala, India. This is where she spent much of her time online comparing their parents and grandparents' stories. She discovered that mostly everyone's desire and life's goal was to go to Tibet.

"*How can we get there?*" Yangchen asked. And every time the answer was the same from everyone. "*We cannot.*" She was not happy but the more she was told no, the more she was determined to somehow go there. Someway.

CHAPTER TWO

AS TIME WENT ON, Yangchen spent less and less time online. She became more disheartened with the disappointment that she was not able to go to Tibet. She became sullen and inward. Her parents addressed the issue with her, and she fluffed it off that she had a lot of pressure trying to decide her future. It was this time that her revered grandfather was extremely ill.

She went to visit him every day at his house next door. She watched him sleep and often checked to make sure he was still breathing. Every so often, when he woke up, she would caress his cheek. One time, his eyes fluttered open.

"I was having a dream that you will one day soon return to Tibet," he said weakly. "When you arrive in Lhasa, see if you can find my friend. He is of the highest sect, known as the Yellow Hat, as am I. His name is Panchen High Lama Kelsang." He fell fast asleep again.

"I will Grandfather," she cooed softly. "I will."

This moment marked a turning point in her mood and was lifted to the point of excitement and determination. Going to Tibet now became her life's goal. She told her parents about it, but they scoffed at the idea. "How can you return?" they asked. "And besides, what is wrong living in Nepal? It is beautiful here, and we have all that we need."

"I like Nepal a lot," Yangchen said convincingly. "But I just want to go. It is for Grandfather." Her parents exchanged wavering glances. They knew their daughter was determined to the point of being stubborn.

It was the next day that her grandfather passed away. A sadness instantly enveloped the household. As the word spread quickly throughout the village, friends and neighbors would drop by to pay their respects for this holy and esteemed man. It was three days of tributes, *sutras,* and chants. Yangchen never left his side for the entire three days. When the last person on the last day said goodbye, Yangchen bent to his stilled body and whispered into his ear, "Rest well, dear Grandfather. And don't worry, I will go to Tibet and say *Tashi Delek* to your friend, Panchen High Lama Kelsang."

On the day of the funeral, hundreds of people gathered in the consecrated burial grounds. Yangchen stood at the front, with prayer hands to her chest, and stayed silent while a tear ran down her cheek as her grandfather was lowered into the ground.

It was late in the afternoon when the family arrived back home. The mood was naturally quiet and somber. At first, the family sat around the main room with no one speaking. Her two younger brothers silently played together. Her sister, three years younger, played with Lucy while her mom prepared *dalbhat* for dinner. Her dad held his father's prayer wheel, spinning in clockwise fashion over and over.

And Yangchen? She took out her phone and went back online to the Tibet refugee chat rooms, and posted a question: *Who will come with me to Tibet?*

Chapter Three

YANGCHEN COULD NOT SLEEP that night. Tossing and turning, her mind raced. Like a mantra, her grandfather's dream resonated. After an hour or so of sleep, she felt her phone vibrate. Instinctively, she reached for it, but it was just out of reach. She inched herself closer to the phone, and sleepily looked what the notification was. Her eyes widened. There were twenty-three responses to her comment in the Tibet refugee chatroom. As she scanned through the messages, she became enthusiastic as the comments were mostly the same:

Yes, we want to go to Tibet too. How to arrange?

She looked up to see if anyone was awake as all were sleeping. She dug deep inside her covers and threw them over her head. The phone's display glowed like a beacon. She thought a moment of what to say. She had so much to say but thought best to keep it simple. Then she tapped out a message reply to the group: *Where does everyone live? I live near Pokhara, Nepal.*

Yangchen stayed with the covers over her head. The house was silent. She stared at her phone for any notifications. Then it vibrated, and she went straight to the messages. *'Dharmshala, India,'* was one response. Then another, *'Bhutan'*, *'Kathmandu'*, *'Pokhara'*, *'Sikkim'*. The responses flowed. She clicked on the profile of this person from Pokhara, who was an old friend who lived in her village but had moved away before high school. His name was Lobsang.

Yangchen thought of what to say. She smiled as she remembered she liked Lobsang when they were younger but had lost track of him. She sent him a friend request, and then clicked on to private messaging, putting her fingers to her mouth and said, "Hmmmm."

'Tashi Delek Lobsang, do you remember me? How are you doing? You want to go to Tibet?'

She stayed underneath her covers, but then their dog, Lucy came to her bed and wanted to play. "Shhh. Not now Lucy, I am busy." Lucy started to growl and began to dig at the covers with her paws.

"Okay, fine."

She threw back her covers, put her phone down, and took Lucy outside for her morning walk. At the last second, she grabbed her phone. At first, her screen was blank, and she decided to focus on Lucy as they slowly meandered on the road outside her home. It was a cloudy, cool morning. Rain was on its way. Suddenly, Lucy bolted and ran down the road with Yangchen frantically following her. When Yangchen caught up to her, Lucy was wagging her tail as an orange and yellow-robed monk sat in prayer fashion. Lucy was so excited to see the monk, as he continued to sit there mindfully unaware of the friendly dog who wanted attention by sniffing the monk. Yangchen took Lucy's collar to head back home. Just then, the monk opened his eyes, placed his hands to heart center, and smiled.

"Come," he said gesturing to Yangchen to sit with him. Yangchen sat by the monk, with her now obedient Lucy by her side. The monk proceeded with a morning blessing, while Yangchen calmly sat there with her eyes closed. He said in English:

"It is beneficial for us that the Blessed One, having passed away for long but leaving the great benefits behind."

Yangchen couldn't believe it. He had to have meant her grandfather. With the prayer over, Yangchen slowly opened her eyes. The monk stared at her serenely.

"How is it you said this prayer today?" she asked.

"I felt it appropriate for your spirit," the monk peacefully responded.

"You have no idea," she said sardonically.

"Oh, but I do have the idea," the monk paused. "This is why I said this prayer."

Yangchen was silent and felt bad for sounding so silly with what she said. Then her phone vibrated. "Excuse me," she said to the monk and looked at her phone. It was a message from Lobsang.

"May I read?" she asked the monk. He blinked his eyes, indicating yes.

'Yes, I remember you. And I do want to go to Tibet. What do you have in mind?'

Yangchen put the phone down and grimaced. She had nothing in mind and knew it would almost be impossible to trek through Tibet to Lhasa.

She shot back a quick message and wrote, *'I don't know. I just need to.'*

She felt a bit down with the awareness that her dream of going was entirely impractical and was dismayed with herself for being such an unrealistic dreamer. But she was happy that another dreamer was now in her life, her old friend Lobsang.

She wrote another quick message. *'Can we meet sometime?'*

'Yes,' came the swift response. She sent a smiley face back to give her some time to think. Then she had an idea.

"Have you ever wanted to go to Tibet?" she asked the monk.

"Yes. Every day I think of going, but it is impossible."

"If I can figure out a way to go, would you come with me?"

The monk sat in stone silence, then closed his eyes to meditate. Not a minute went by when he opened his eyes again. "Yes, young Yangchen, I would join you on this journey."

She looked at him quizzically. "But how did you know my name?"

"You have become known to us at the monastery, for your dream of returning to Tibet."

"But I haven't told anyone about it," she said as a matter of fact.

"Ah, yes. I responded to your *Return to Tibet* post," the monk said. Yangchen was impressed with herself and smiled.

"But you are on social media?" she asked surprised.

The monk placed his hands to heart center. "Come to the monastery and drink some butter tea with us some time," the monk offered.

"Yes, I would like that," Yangchen bowed in thankfulness.

Yangchen stood and told Lucy to come, and they unhurriedly walked back to her house, the monk watched as she slipped below the horizon.

Chapter Four

Everyone was stirring around to prepare breakfast. Lucy checked her bowl for breakfast too. Yangchen went to her bed to check the phone again. There was a message from Lobsang, but she couldn't read it just yet.

"Yangchen," her mom called out. "Come. Breakfast."

There was a space on the floor with colorful patterned carpets, blankets, Tibetan handmade carpets where the family always had their meals. Yangchen was the last to join while they ate their daily *tsampa,* a hearty mix of roasted barley mixed with tea and yak milk. And a small cup of *po cha*, or butter tea. The family sat around quietly in mourning for their sacred family member. Yangchen was first to break the silence.

"I met a monk this morning," Yangchen said to anyone willing to listen. The room remained subdued. Everyone was silently sipping their tea, and a bite here and there of the tsampa. She was attempting to lighten the mood despite her own sadness for the loss of her beloved grandfather. She continued.

"Uh, yeh. He invited me to his monastery. I remember we all went when we were kids."

"You're still kids," her father said affectionately, responding to his eldest daughter. She smiled.

Yangchen felt her hunger and gobbled up the tsampa and drank the butter tea in one gulp.

"You were hungry," her mom commented. Yangchen nodded. Her two younger brothers quietly played together while her sister daintily sipped the tea as if she were the Queen of England. She looked over at her elder sister.

"I would like to come to the monastery with you," Pema asked.

"No, no. I am going alone, Pema," Yangchen said firmly yet kindly to her younger sister. Pema looked disappointed.

"What is so important at this monastery, Yangchen?" her father asked.

"Uh...nothing," Yangchen responded nonchalantly. "Just to see what it's like, I guess."

"That is fine, daughter...you may visit. You are eighteen now and can make your own destiny."

"Destiny. Yes," she said, pondering and repeating a couple times. "Destiny. I like that word. I shall use it often. Thank you, my dear father." She stood and went over to him and gave him a big hug.

"I want to do great things with my destiny."

***

Yangchen remembered that Lobsang's message was waiting for her.

'Yangchen, I want to see you again.'

She was excited with the prospect of seeing her friend once more. It had been so long. She remembered she liked him a lot. Now she was eighteen, and even her father said to form her own destiny. Yangchen felt confident.

'Can you come here?' she asked Lobsang. *'There is someone I want you to meet.'*

No response. Silence from her phone was making her crazy. Often the mobile network was weak or not working at all, which made communication difficult and frustrating. Yangchen sat in her bed, clutching her phone as if her life depended on it. It dawned on her too that waiting was not good. She lovingly gazed at her mom, who was cleaning up in the kitchen.

"What can I do, mom? To help, I mean?"

"Please. I need half kg of yak cheese from the market. Just look after your brothers and play with them. Your sister too."

"Come on," Yangchen said making a big swooping arm gesture to get them out the door. "You too Lucy."

The clouds from early this morning had burned off and the day had warmed up, the sun shining high in the sky. The distinctive towering and sacred Machapucchre peak glistened as did the entire Annapurna range that surrounds this beautiful hamlet. Yangchen told her siblings to stop for a minute for a look.

"See?" she pointed. "Look how pretty this view is." The boys playfully mocked their older sister.

"We have seen, elder sister…many times."

She paid them no mind and slowly walked on towards the center of the village. "Come on," she said, attempting to keep them in tow. As they walked by, neighbors would stop in their tracks and bow to the four kids, in honor of their grandfather. The four would bow in return.

Yangchen had a sudden spasm in her belly that her time in the village and her family home was short-lived. She felt a sadness for this idea, and yet excitement that she was on the verge of an adventure of a lifetime. Her sister pointed out the Buddhist monastery.

"Is that where you will visit?" Pema asked.

"Yes, but not now," Yangchen responded.

"I know…not now," Pema said disheartened.

Yangchen saw the monk she had spoken with just outside the Monastery earlier in the morning. He placed his hands to heart center, and she placed hers as well, and smiled. She interpreted this as a sign, some sort of meaning for her quest. The four walked on to a market to purchase the yak cheese. When Yangchen asked the proprietor for half kg, he told her there would be no charge.

"In honor of your grandfather. Tashi delek," he kindly told her.

"*Tujay chay*. Thank you," Yangchen said.

When they left the market, Pema turned to her sister. "Grandfather was very known here, wasn't he?" she asked.

"Yes, sister dear. He was an important man."

"Are we ever going to go to Tibet?" Pema asked. Yangchen quizzically examined her up and down. She thought it was very curious Pema would ask her such a question.

"I don't know…maybe," Yangchen answered unenthusiastically. Pema ignored her answer.

"If you go, I will go too," Pema said defiantly.

"We'll see," Yangchen said firmly.

The kids walked back to the house with a quicker pace this time, led by Yangchen. She had left her phone at the house and was hoping there was a message from Lobsang. The more she thought about him, the more she realized he could help her in her mission of successfully crossing the border and marching all the way to Lhasa.

Upon returning to their house, Yangchen practically ran to her phone. Still no message from Lobsang. "Grrrrr," she growled with disappointment. "Oh, mom, here is the yak cheese. The man said we didn't need to pay for it. In honor of grandfather." Her mom smiled.

Yangchen went to her bed and curled into a ball. Her mood was suddenly gloomy. She was sad for the loss of her grandfather. She was sad she had not heard from Lobsang. And she was sad her plan, for now, had stalled.

CHAPTER FIVE

HAVING SLEPT ALL THE way till dinner, Yangchen awoke groggy and hungry. She continued to idly lay down in her bed. Reaching over for her phone, she found a message from Lobsang.

'I will try to catch a ride to your village. You still live in the same house?'

Yangchen sat bolt upright and started to slightly hyperventilate. "Oh my God." Her mom, who was preparing the evening meal, heard.

"Are you okay, Yangchen?" She didn't realize she had made some commotion. Theirs was a small house, having one room with a small side kitchen and bathroom. Nothing was easily concealed and held private, except in the wee hours of the night under the covers.

"Ummm, yah mom. My old friend Lobsang is coming to visit. Can he stay here?" Momentary silence followed. Yangchen left her bed and came over to her mom. "Can he, mom?"

"Who is he?"

"Lobsang. He lived here, but his family moved away somewhere. He and I were really good friends years ago." Her mom remained preoccupied, making steamed dumplings, called momos. "So, can he?"

"Space is limited dear, you know that."

"That's okay, he can sleep in my bed." Her mom gave her an intimidating look. "I mean, I wouldn't sleep in my bed too. I can sleep with Pema, or something."

"We will ask your father when he gets home."

Yangchen went back to her bed to tap out a quick reply.

'I am asking my parents if you can stay here. When are you going to come?"

Yangchen needed to pace herself knowing replies were not usually immediate. She just sat there thinking that having a phone is good but also stressful. She wondered if it would always be like this. But her phone vibrated catching her by surprise.

'I can come real soon. Just let me know if it is okay to stay at your house.'

She looked over to her mom, her mouth half-open, but the situation would be the same. Only when her father comes back home.

Yangchen's father did not work anymore. Most days, he would spend time drinking butter tea with other Tibetan refugees who had come with their parents and grandparents from Tibet; or born in Nepal, but their Tibetan blood was impermeable. They too often discussed if there would ever be the right time to cross over. Plus, they were getting on in years, and such an undertaking would be physically punishing having to cross the many high passes and extremely dangerous. At best, they would end up in Tibet prison. At worst, they could die. Whenever they could find a newspaper, they would all take turns scouring for any news about anything that mattered most to them: the opportunity. But there never was as their hopes to return were dim.

They were consigned to the reality; Nepal was their home and they could only worship holy Lhasa from afar.

When Dorje, Yangchen's father arrived home, he admitted to having a couple of glasses of *chang*, the Tibetan beer made of barley. He felt happy, naturally, and Yangchen caught wind of this immediately.

"Father dear. I have a friend who wants to visit. Can he stay here, please?" She gave him a hug. "Oh, thank you!" she said exuberantly.

"I did not bless this." At first, her father was annoyed. But shortly, he calmed down. "Who is this friend?"

"He used to live here in the village and then moved away. He wants to come with me to the monastery." Pausing for a moment to catch her breath, she continued.

"Can he stay, pleaseeeee?"

"Yes, dearest Yangchen, he may stay. I can never say no to you."

"Thank you, daddy."

The first thing Yangchen did was to write to Lobsang and tell him that he was invited to stay at her house.

Lobsang wrote back right away, as if he was hovering over his phone anxiously waiting.

'Great. I will make arrangements and let you know when I can come, but it will be soon.'

She sent him a smiley.

***

Days had gone by as Yangchen had not heard from Lobsang. She tried to remain calm and stay busy doing various chores to help around the house, and to mind after her brothers and sister. And to play with the spirited Lucy. With the eventual arrival of Lobsang, it was a symbolic visit to not only explore their relationship but also the potential of her mission of crossing into Tibet.

She re-read her sacred Joan of Arc story to give her courage. Yangchen felt she needed it as the eventual crossing would not only be an arduous journey, beset with so many possible dangers from animals, the elements, and the ever-present Chinese army. She would have self-doubts about even attempting the crossing. She even thought it was kind of crazy, but her grandfather's words gave her the inspiration to do it. She kept all this quiet to her family, as she knew they would not approve. They wouldn't even let her out of the house if they knew.

In the afternoon, she took a solo walk up to the monastery to see if she could find her monk friend to let him know she would want to have a visit, and she would be bringing a friend. But it was prayer time as she stood out front, listening to the resonating Buddhist chants. It was a dreamy, mystical sound that always made her feel at peace, and just the right sound at the right time.

Suddenly, her phone vibrated with Lobsang's message:

'I can arrive tomorrow.'
'Yeh! See you tomorrow.'

CHAPTER SIX

THE NEXT DAY, THE rains returned with a vengeance. The pounding sound on the tin roof reverberated, shaking the house. Yangchen nervously paced around. Lucy followed her every step. "Stop following me," Yangchen said tensely, out of her ordinary spirit. Lucy went to lie down in her pillow, her tail between her legs. Yangchen felt bad. She went over to Lucy. "I'm sorry, Lucy," she said, and patted her on the head. Lucy wagged her tail and issued a soft, friendly bark.

Just then, there was a quiet knock on the door. The symbolic knock that meant her life would never be the same again. Her heart raced and she ran to the door.

"Who is it?" she playfully asked. Of course, it was Lobsang. When the door opened, they both pressed their hands to their chest issuing a silent tashi delek and smiled. The pleasant-looking Lobsang was soaking wet.

"You have changed," Yangchen said.

"So have you," Lobsang said with a deeper eighteen-year-old voice. Yangchen giggled.

"Your voice has changed too," she said still smiling.

She invited him inside their house. Lobsang looked all around while Lucy came to smell and greet him. The rest of her family stood, waiting to be introduced. Yangchen's mom went to get a towel for Lobsang.

"Do you remember my family?"

"Yes, kind of," Lobsang said unassuredly while wiping the rainwater out of his eyes. "But your bothers hadn't been born yet." Yangchen nodded. "Umm, actually can I change my clothes? I am very wet."

"Yes, bathroom is there," Yangchen pointed towards the way. Lobsang reached into his smallish backpack for dry clothes. It was wrapped in a plastic bag to prevent it from getting wet. He found a dry pair of pants and shirt and went to the bathroom to change and emerged within a minute.

"Come, please sit. Mom is preparing tea," Yangchen directed. Lobsang, just being reacquainted, felt a bit nervous. Yangchen sensed this.

"I am happy you are here," Yangchen sweetly said. Lobsang smiled.

"Me too."

Dorje, her father, stayed quiet, but only for a moment.

"Tell me Lobsang, how is your family?" Dorje asked. Lobsang briefly glanced over to Yangchen looking for reassurance. She half smiled with a slight nod.

"They are good, sir," he said. "We live a simple life."

"Yes, so do we. It is Tibetan refugee life in Nepal. Pleasant and simple."

Yangchen's mom brought cups of butter tea for everyone. She handed Lobsang his tea. He was still a bit cold from the rain, and a bit nervous. With his hands a bit shaky, he accidentally spilled some of the tea on the carpet.

"Oh no, I'm so sorry," Lobsang said with regret.

"Not to worry, we have spilled many times," her father said with a smile and laugh. "Enough times of spilling for many meals and many cups of tea." He gave Lobsang a reassuring and approving glance. He already saw that Lobsang made his daughter happy. Any potential suiter for his daughter that he approved of made him happy too. "There is good karma in this room," her dad stated.

"How was your journey here?" Yangchen asked. "It was long and bumpy, but I am happy to be here," Lobsang answered.

"You look happy that your friend is here, Yangchen," her dad commented.

"Yes, daddy, I am," she said compassionately. She shyly looked over to Lobsang.

"I do remember you and Lobsang played together all the time when he lived in our village," her dad commented. He looked at Lobsang, "I also remember you were polite." Yangchen smiled. "He's still polite, Daddy," she spoke as she rolled her eyes.

He was poured another cup of tea and the entire family, including her two brothers, sister, and Lucy all quietly sat around while the rain continued to pound their corrugated metal roof. It was a loud deafening sound which made hearing each other difficult. They all knew to wait for the rain to lighten up to speak again. Yangchen's mom brought out a plate of tsampa to munch on until dinner. Lobsang was handed the plate first, as guests are always served first. He took a bite to swirl around in his mouth and then popped the rest of it in his mouth. Before the rest of the family took theirs, he was offered another.

"It seems you have not eaten in a while," her father commented.

"Yes sir, not since early this morning." He popped the second one in his mouth. He was offered a third. "No, no, please. You eat," Lobsang said good manneredly.

Her mom passed the plate around, and soon, everyone was quietly munching away.

"These are really good," Lobsang said addressing Yangchen's mom. "Something is different than what my mom makes."

"Yangchen made them for you," her mom said. Lobsang looked over to Yangchen, who was beaming a broad smile. "I put cinnamon in them," Yangchen said. "It adds a little more flavor and taste."

"Cinnamon, yes I can taste it now." Yangchen handed the plate for Lobsang to take a third. "Yes, please...I guess I am hungry." Lobsang sheepishly took one more tsampa, and in two bites, he swallowed it. Yangchen's dad looked over to Lobsang, as silence was still the decree, despite the rain having lessoned some.

"Tell me, Lobsang," Dorje asked. "Why exactly have you come?" Lobsang looked over to Yangchen for direction, or something, since the two had agreed not to bring up their secret plan.

"Yangchen invited me to come and visit the monastery here." Yangchen's dad looked a bit skeptical.

"But you have a monastery in your village," Dorje said. Lobsang looked over to Yangchen for support.

"I told him to come see this monastery, daddy, and to meet this monk that is there...the one I told you about I met the other day."

"And what is so special about this monk?" Dorje asked. Yangchen was quiet, as was Lobsang.

"I don't know, he was nice and invited me to visit. I thought Lobsang would want to come." Pema spoke up. "I told Yangchen I wanted to come too."

Yangchen shot her a menacing glance to be quiet. "We'll see," Yangchen said. Pema lost her enthusiasm and remained quiet.

Yangchen tenderly looked over to Lobsang. They held their glances for more than a moment. She felt a growing affection for him. Finally, she spoke.

"We will visit the monastery tomorrow."

CHAPTER SEVEN

UNSURPRISINGLY, HARD RAIN POUNDED their roof waking everyone up. Lucy was already at the front door to go outside, so Yangchen let her out for a few minutes. When she returned, she was soaking wet and shook herself off scattering water droplets everywhere. Yangchen poured some food into her bowl, and Lucy gobbled it up.

The rest of the family stirred and slowly got out of bed. Lobsang, who was set up to sleep in a corner, was still sleeping. Yangchen went over to wake him up.

"Wake up sleepyhead, today is a big day." Lobsang smiled, rubbing his eyes.

"Yes, a big day," he said sleepily.

"It is raining a lot. We can have breakfast and wait for the rain to calm down," Yangchen explained to Lobsang.

After breakfast, the rain did subside, and the two ventured outside for the short trek to the monastery. As they approached, they could hear the monks chanting.

"I love that sound," Yangchen told him.

"Me too," Lobsang responded.

They entered inside the large grounds of the monastery compound, climbing the steps to enter inside. There, they found the great hall where the monks were chanting. Deep, resonating voices recited Buddhist scriptures. Then cymbals crashed, and *dungchen*, or long horns blew. Yangchen scanned the room for her friend. She didn't see him just yet.

"I don't even know his name. Silly me, I didn't ask."

"It's okay Yangchen, we will find him," Lobsang said reassuring her.

She smiled and liked his calm, comforting ways. They slowly walked around the room, looking at each face. At one point, Yangchen wasn't sure she would identify him. She hoped he would recognize her. Suddenly, all the cymbals and horns stopped to a complete and total silence. Yangchen and Lobsang stopped in their tracks. All the monks' heads were lowered in prayer. Movement started to happen, and from behind, Yangchen's friend approached, pleasantly startling her.

"I am happy you have come, young Yangchen," the monk said. He bowed and placed his hands to his chest. Yangchen and Lobsang reciprocated in kind.

"This is my friend Lobsang," Yangchen introduced him to the monk.

"My name is Chen-tao. It means true guide." Chen-tao bowed, and again, Yangchen and Lobsang bowed in kind. All three stood in silence for a moment or two.

"Come," Chen-tao said. "Let us speak."

Yangchen and Lobsang followed Chen-tao into a small room off the main room. He signaled a younger monk to prepare tea. The three sat down on the floor in lotus position and remained silent while waiting for the tea. The young monk arrived with a big pot of tea and three small cups, and delicately poured the butter tea filling the cups to the rim. They quietly sipped the hot tea. Finally, the silence was broken.

"How is your sadness for your grandfather, Yangchen?" Chen-tao asked. Yangchen frowned at the thought of her beloved grandfather, and at first, hesitated speaking.

"Of course, I am sad. I loved him so much, and he loved me too. For this, I will always cherish his memory."

Lobsang looked surprised at this news.

"Oh, I am so sorry for your loss, Yangchen. I did not know."

"Yes. He passed away last week," she said saddened. "Right before he passed, he told me he had a dream I came to Tibet." Silence reigned for a few moments, as they sipped their tea. A tear ran down her cheek. Trying to stop her emotion, she made that sound of attempting not to cry.

"I told him I would do all I can to go…for him, and to say Tashi Delek to anyone I meet, and especially his friend, High Lama." Chen-tao looked over to Yangchen. "I will come with you." Suddenly, the concept of crossing became very real to both Yangchen and Lobsang. Yangchen looked over to Lobsang.

"We haven't spoken about this, Lobsang. Why do you want to go?" Yangchen asked. Lobsang looked down at the teacup he held in both hands. He too became emotional.

"My father also passed away last year," he said. "And he asked me the same, that I go to Tibet. I want to fulfill his dream. He was never able to go, like all refugees." Silence again. It was a very emotional moment. Finally, Chen-tao spoke.

"I too have a reason. My father is held in prison in Lhasa. I want to try and free him." Both Lobsang and Yangchen looked over to the sad monk. "Then we all have good reasons to go," Yangchen said eagerly. "When can we go?" she asked. Chen-tao shook his head.

"We cannot cross now. It is monsoon. We cannot cross after as it will be winter." They all took the last sips of their tea.

"We can cross in spring."

CHAPTER EIGHT

TEN YEARS AGO

THE CHINESE SOLDIER, LI and the Tibetan woman Tenzin met for tea. It was their first meeting since the passing of her mother. Initially, sitting together was awkward. Not for them being uncomfortable together. But for the unapproving stares they would receive from both Tibetan patrons and other Chinese soldiers. They quickly learned to ignore everyone around them. They knew that theirs was an unusual association. Be it the mysterious laws of attraction or some other higher force at play, whatever reason, they felt contented and natural together.

Sipping their tea in comfortable silences, Tenzin started to mouth a couple of words, but stopped.

"Please," he said with assurance. "Tell me what you would like to say." Tenzin looked down for a moment, then straightened her posture.

"I want to thank you again for helping my *amala*," she softly said. "My mother." Li nodded an approving smile. "It was a natural reaction to help." Her hands were in her lap, and he reached with his hands, to ask for hers. She obliged, and sitting there, holding hands, he told her his confession.

"I had seen you many times," he spoke as he began to swallow back emotion. "I wanted to say hello so many times, but I did not know how to." Tenzin sat in joyous silence, smiling. "I too have seen you many times," she confessed.

"But I never saw you look at me," Li responded. Then his face brightened. "Except for that one time." Tenzin smiled.

"I always look the other way," she responded, smiling. "Yes, except for that one time."

"*Jingya de*," he said. She had a quizzical look. "It means surprised."

"Surprised?" Tenzin asked.

"I was surprised you finally looked at me," he said humbly. They each took a couple sips of tea.

"Tenzin, I must tell you something." He paused for a moment and held her hands a bit firmer. "My time and post here is temporary in Lhasa. In a few months, I will need to leave back to Beijing." At first, Tenzin was disappointed, but then her eyes brightened.

"Buddhist philosophy says that the path to no suffering is unattachment." Pausing for a moment, she continued, "But it is too late."

"What do you mean?" he asked. Tenzin did not respond. Li didn't force it.

They sat sipping tea and felt such comfort in their silence. Finally, Li broke their silence.

"Can I take you to dinner tonight?"

"Yes, I would like that very much."

***

They arranged to meet at a restaurant next to the tea shop at 6 PM. Li arrived a little early, and found a table facing the door. Minutes passed. He became a bit edgy, as he contemplated Tenzin's arrival. *The night always has the potential for greater possibilities*, he thought. *Further confessions and stories, and maybe even a little romance, too*. He kept looking at the clock on his phone, and as he set it down, Tenzin walked through the door. Li thought she looked exquisite, wearing a bright red *chupa*, her long dark hair bordering her beautiful face. It was clear, Li was enamored by her. She smiled as she saw him sitting at the table, and gracefully walked over to him. He stood to welcome her and assisted with her seat in as she sat down.

"You look so beautiful," Li said. She gushed and blushed a bit, shyly looking down. But that didn't last long. The waiter brought a steaming plate of momos to the table.

"I ordered momos. Please have."

"Yes, I am quite hungry actually," Tenzin said, and took one, dipping it in the savory sauce provided. Li followed. After finishing the first one, Tenzin looked over to Li.

"I am happy you like Tibetan food."

"I do. So different from Chinese food."

"I can make momos with my eyes closed," she said smiling.

"I would like to try them."

The waiter came over to take the rest of their order.

"Please Tenzin, choose what you like, I can eat everything."

"We want *thukpa* please," Tenzin told the waiter. Li quickly scanned the menu to look for a description.

"Oh, that sounds good, good choice. Soup."

"Tibetan soup. It is our national dish. All Tibetan people like it."

Finishing the plate of momos, Li looked over to Tenzin.

"Tenzin, I have something else to tell you." She nodded munching on the last momo. "Something you should know."

"My father is very high up in the Chinese government. He will become the Supreme Leader one day."

Tenzin half-smiled, barely acknowledging what Li had just told her. Li continued, although a bit perplexed at Tenzin's relaxed response. Maybe she didn't understand, he thought.

"Yes, he is a good man, and supportive of what I do. I am his and my mother's only child."

Tenzin took a sip of water. "I am an only child too. In fact, I am the only person of my family now," she said a bit downhearted.

"Oh, that is sad."

"Since my *amala* has passed, I am lost for what to do with my life. I was even thinking of leaving Tibet for... somewhere...but I don't know where." She became lost in thought. Li listened intently; his mind raced with wild thoughts. Finally, he spoke.

"Tenzin, I know we are new to each other, but I feel we both share the same feelings."

She happily nodded in agreement.

"Attraction is an interesting thing," Li said. Tenzin keenly listened. "I find you to be quietly simple. And so beautiful. I feel at peace with you."

"I find you to be noble and brave and kind."

"Only that?" Li smiled a mischievous smile. She studied his face. Then nodded a slight nod.

"I like your eyes. Here is where I find kindness," she said. "In your eyes." Li smiled.

Their meal arrived at the table, one big pot and two bowls. Tenzin dished out two bowls full. Neither hesitated to begin. "This is so good, Tenzin."

They sat quietly while persistently eating until their bowls were clean. They both looked at each other with pure satisfaction on their faces, while signaling they were ready to leave. They quietly walked on to the bustling streets, hand in hand. They continued to receive odd stares, but again they chose to ignore them. Li led them down a quiet street. It was his intention. He turned towards Tenzin and announced his intentions.

"I am going to kiss you now." She didn't flinch. Li was just a couple inches taller and leaned in giving Tenzin a kiss. It lasted for more than a few seconds, and they both thoroughly enjoyed it. Li pulled back allowing for them to breathe.

"I have a confession," she said. "I have never kissed before." Li smiled.

"I have a confession too," he said. "This is my first time kissing too." She smiled. He leaned in and kissed her again. This time deeper and longer, and by the end of this kiss, they were madly in love.

CHAPTER NINE

WHEN YANGCHEN AND LOBSANG said goodbye to Chen-tao, the skies had cleared. They slowly walked back towards Yangchen's home. But they weren't in any hurry. They had many months to wait to put their plan into action.

"What are we going to do till spring?" Yangchen asked Lobsang.

"We wait, Yangchen," Lobsang said. "We just need to be patient and wait." Lobsang took Yangchen's hand. She smiled and felt her blood excitedly rush through her body. She had never felt the warm touch of a boy. She liked it.

"You know something?" Lobsang asked.

"Yes," Yangchen said.

"Yes, what?" Lobsang asked.

"I know something," she replied giggling.

"What do you know?" he asked.

"I know you like me," she said cooing.

"Umm, yes, that is what I was going to say," he said. "I like you."

"I like you too, Lobsang."

They continued down the road to her house, hand in hand. Perhaps the disappointment of having to wait was tempered by their newly founded relation. Before reaching her home, Lobsang turned to Yangchen, and gave her a quick kiss.

"I like you a lot, actually," Lobsang whispered. Yangchen grinned and felt genuinely happy. Yangchen broke her hand free, starting to run, shouted, "I'll race you to the house." Lobsang followed and caught up to Yangchen's headstart but slowed at the end when they reached her house.

"Awww, that's no fair," Yangchen said. "You let me win."

"No, I didn't, you are fast!"

It was late afternoon when they entered the house. No one was home, even Lucy.

"I wonder where they went?" Yangchen asked. "I'll make tea."

While Yangchen went to prepare tea, Lobsang walked around the tidy house, and looked at some of the pictures on the wall. "You have a nice family, Yangchen."

"I like them," she said as she brought tea into the sitting area.

"My family is small, just my mom and me," he said wistfully.

As they sat drinking tea, Yangchen furrowed her brow. "When we go to Tibet, you will be leaving your mom alone."

"I thought of that," he responded.

"Is it okay?"

"I don't know," he said. "In fact, not really."

"Then maybe you shouldn't go," she said.

"No, no. I want to go," he said reassuring her.

"Are you sure?"

"Yes, I am sure."

They silently sipped their tea.

"We need to prepare for this trip, Yangchen," Lobsang said. "We need to get a map, study some books, and start to get things we will need. It is a long journey."

"I don't have any money to buy anything," she pleaded.

"Me neither," Lobsang. "But we have six months or more to figure that out."

Finishing the last of their tea, Yangchen spoke up. "We need to find a way to make some money, like selling Tibetan handicrafts to tourists down in Pokhara."

"Great idea!" Lobsang exclaimed.

***

When Yangchen's family returned, she pounced all over her dad. But her dad spoke first.

"You may stay for dinner, Lobsang, but tomorrow you must leave for your home."

"No dad, we..." Her dad interrupted her. "I am sure Lobsang's dear mother would like to have him back," her dad responded. "Yes," Yangchen countered. "But we have a plan to go to Pokhara and sell Tibetan things to tourists. We need to make money." He suspiciously looked at her.

"For what? You have what you need." Yangchen looked over to Lobsang and shook her head.

"I want to get stuff, you know...stuff."

"Stuff," her dad said gruffly. "You are Buddhist, Yangchen. Stuff is not important."

"Yes, but I'm also a teenage girl...we like stuff." Her dad shook his head, grumbling to himself.

"Okay, okay" her dad sighed. "I know some Tibet craft makers in our village. They can loan you the things, and you pay her back and keep the profits. Maybe it is a good idea, you learn business."

"Thank you, daddy," Yangchen said. "But Lobsang wants to come too. Can he stay a few more days?" He turned to Lobsang. "Lobsang, you may stay for some days, but after that you will need to go back home." Lobsang pressed his hands together to heart center in appreciation. Her dad shook his head but knew whatever his oldest daughter wanted, he usually gave in.

"We'll go see her tomorrow to arrange your Tibetan things selling. And yes, with Lobsang." Yangchen grinned and winked at Lobsang.

Chapter Ten

THE NEXT MORNING, YANGCHEN'S dad escorted her and Lobsang to a nearby neighbor who made Tibetan crafts such as bracelets, amulets, Buddhist carvings, and the like. She was very generous and gave Yangchen about twenty-five pieces, all labeled with her cost. She explained to remove the tag before letting any tourists see the cost and add her profit.

"Whatever you can negotiate for," she said. "You keep profit after my cost."

"This is going to be fun," Yangchen said with enthusiasm.

"Go to Lakeside where tourists are," her dad said. Yangchen nodded her head. "I know where to go," she said confidently.

The day was amazingly clear for the monsoon season, and they took a bus down to Lakeside. They found a convenient place to set up their little shop. Yangchen brought a white cloth to lay down on the cement surface and laid out all the things by category. And then sat there.

A few tourists walked by, but mostly paid them no attention. Yangchen would even wave over to tourists as they passed, or even discreetly call over to them. Any tourist could buy any of these things in the multiple tourists shop just up the road that led to the main part of town. She and Lobsang exchanged apprehensive glances.

"Maybe this won't be so easy," Yangchen commented.

"Be patient, Yangchen," Lobsang said. "We just started."

They sat there for a couple more hours, as the morning slipped into the afternoon. Monsoon clouds started to form. "I think we better go home, Lobsang, before it rains." But a tourist approached them and asked to see their things.

"Please, have a look," Yangchen said inviting him. He looked but then turned to walk away. Yangchen turned her head. "Maybe we need to think of another way to make money," she said.

"Don't give up so easily," Lobsang tried to encourage her. "Plus, this is monsoon season and not as many tourists."

Storm clouds started to build even more. Yangchen and Lobsang packed up their belongings, placing them in Yangchen's backpack and walked to the bus stop to catch a one-hour bus ride up the hill to their village. When they arrived home, her mom and dad were curious if they were successful. Yangchen disappointedly shook her head.

"Yangchen," her dad said with scorn. "You dress like westerners with your athlete clothes." Yangchen looked down at herself. "But I am comfortable, daddy."

"I suggest you wear *chuba* next time," her dad said. "You are a Tibetan girl and should look Tibetan. Foreign tourists like Tibet. I am sure they will see you and get more foreigners to buy." Lobsang also wore western clothes. "And Lobsang, you can use my *chuba*."

"Thank you, sir." He addressed Yangchen's dad pressing his hands together.

Yangchen looked at her phone to get the next day's weather. It forecasted to be clear in the morning and rain in the afternoon. "Tomorrow, we try again wearing Tibetan clothes."

***

The next day, Lobsang and Yangchen left early in the morning to catch the maximum time down by Lakeside before the next storm. When they set up their little shop, they were ready to welcome foreigners to see their ornamental inventory, and hopefully, buy something. Both Yangchen and Lobsang were wearing their chubas. "These clothes feel so tight," Yangchen said. "I feel like I'm wrapped in a blanket." Lobsang smiled. "Maybe so. But you look like a Tibetan girl."

A couple of western people approached them, said hello, and looked at their wares. The western girl picked up a beaded bracelet with a little Buddha head as the centerpiece. "Let me help you try it on," Yangchen said. Yangchen placed it around the girl's wrist and closed the clasp. The western girl looked at it admiringly, shaking her wrist to feel for looseness and comfort.

"Oh, I like it," the western girl said. "How much is it?" Yangchen looked at Lobsang, and he nodded his head encouraging Yangchen to close the sale. "It costs eight hundred rupees," responded Yangchen.

The western girl shook her head. "Hmmm, too much," she said. "Five hundred rupees," the western girl countered. Yangchen shook her head, aware of her cost of five hundred rupees.

"I know eight hundred rupees is not a lot of money in your western world. But you will feel good karma always wearing this bracelet. "I give you for seven hundred fifty rupees," Yangchen answered. "Remember, good karma for you."

The western girl nodded to agree and took out her wallet and pulled out a huge stack of thousand-rupee notes. She furrowed her brow. "Hmmm, I don't have change, do you?" Yangchen shook her head no. "Okay," the western girl said. "I give you one thousand, for good karma."

Yangchen nodded and smiled and pressed her hands to her chest. "Thank you." The western girl's boyfriend also looked at the Buddha bracelet, and tried it on too. "That is good, double good karma," Yangchen said. The western guy didn't even try to negotiate and handed Yangchen one thousand rupees for the bracelet. She was ecstatic. "Thank you, thank you." She held all the money in her hands and brought them to her forehead for a blessing.

The western couple said goodbye. Lobsang sat there admiring Yangchen and her sales ability. "Yangchen, you just made one thousand rupees profit!"

"I know. This *chuba* is bringing really good karma," Yangchen said. "My daddy is so smart."

"And so are you, Yangchen."

Arriving home, Yangchen was all smiles. She held the thousand rupees in her hand, and proudly showed them to her family. "Look!" Her father was so surprised. "Imagine what you can make during high tourist season?" he relayed.

"You were so right, I will wear this *chuba*," she said. She excused herself to change into her regular athlete clothes. Her father approached Lobsang while Yangchen went to change.

"How did she do this, Lobsang?" he asked.

"She has charm, sir," he said. "And she is good at selling and knows how to win the hearts of the tourists." Her father nodded his head.

"She has always been that way. Stubborn but convincing…and determined." Lobsang nodded his head in agreement. "I came to know this, and even when I knew her before," Lobsang said. "It is why I like her, sir." Yangchen's father affectionately touched his shoulder. Yangchen emerged from the bathroom.

"I'm going to check the weather for tomorrow. I want to do this again. It was so fun."

CHAPTER ELEVEN

TEN YEARS AGO

LI AND TENZIN ENJOYED a wonderful and dreamy courtship. They would spend all his free time together. They toured the Potala Palace, having walked all throughout, multi-floored and mysterious. Another time, they toured the stately gardens and grounds of Norbulingka, the Dalai Lama's summer home. They would have dinner most nights together. They would eat out, or lately, Tenzin would invite Li over for dinner as he was able to sample her wonderful cooking of all dishes Tibetan. Li grew to love Tibetan food and loved her cooking the best.

After a few months of steady dating, Li had built up enough courage to announce something special. He told Tenzin the night before to prepare something special as she made *thukpa*, his favorite Tibetan dish. At first, Li kept it simple as they talked about their day. He had the day off and did not see Tenzin as she performed her daily circumambulation around the Jokhang. She bought food in the Barkhor to prepare for their special dinner.

Towards the conclusion of their dinner, Li's face grew subdued. Tenzin was concerned. She asked him if everything was okay.

"Everything is fine and perfect," he reassured her. "In fact, I have something to ask you."

"What is it, my dear?" she asked. Li hesitated for a moment and took something out of his pocket but held it below the table. Tenzin was curious.

"I want you to marry me," he said in a serious tone. Tenzin did a double-take and tried to catch her breath. She covered both hands to her mouth. She was so surprised.

"Is it certain?" was her only verbal reaction.

"Yes. It is certain," Li said encouraging her. "I love you, Tenzin." Tenzin smiled.

"I love you too." Li smiled and felt a huge sense of relief.

"But there is one thing," he said as his face grew somber again. "You would need to live with me in Beijing." Tenzin's face was glum. Li wanted to reassure her.

"Do not worry, Tenzin, Tibet's people are protected by Han Chinese, and many Tibetan people live in Beijing," Li reassured her. "You can make friends there." Tenzin was deep in thought, forecasting out what life would be like for her in this new huge city. But in the end, she concluded that she could not live her life without her Chinese soldier.

"Yes, yes," she said. "I will marry you." He took her hands and handed her a small jewelry box. She opened it and saw a nice shiny diamond ring nestled in the velvet box. She took the ring out of the box, and he held his hand out to take the ring and placed it on her ring finger.

"It is beautiful," she cooed. "Just promise me one thing," Tenzin whispered. "Help me free my people."

Li stood from the table, as Tenzin did too, and came around to her side, embraced her and kissed her.

"I will. And we will have a happy life together."

CHAPTER TWELVE

AFTER A SUCCESSION OF inconsistent sales days, the monsoon settled in for the season. Traveling down to Pokhara's Lakeside would prove to be pointless. On the bus back to Yangchen's village, Lobsang turned to her.

"Yangchen, we cannot come here until the monsoon season is over."

"I know," she responded.

"And I need to go home, and be with my mom," Lobsang stated.

"I also know," Yangchen said. "But you will come back in October after monsoon?" she asked.

"Yes, I will," he said. "Save this money, put it in a safe place."

"I will, but I know we need more, much more," she said.

When they arrived back home, Lobsang announced to Yangchen's family that he would leave the next day.

"We enjoyed having you here, Lobsang," Yangchen's father said. "You are welcome here again."

"Thank you, sir," Lobsang said. "I will return in October for the next tourist season."

* * *

Yangchen was sad to see Lobsang leave as she grew close with him. He was also her partner for their plan. And now the monsoon would keep them mostly indoors for months until October. After a sad goodbye, Yangchen went to the Tibet refugee group online since she had not checked it lately, despite the many numerous notifications that had accumulated. She read them all and then responded. One message was from a Tibetan refugee in Bhutan. This person, a girl wrote that she was desperate to go to Lhasa to visit a relative who was sick. Yangchen wrote to her and said that they would coordinate a spring departure, and to save money for this trip and not to cross alone. She wrote back to Yangchen that her elder brother would accompany her. And to stay in touch.

Another person from Dharmshala, India wrote that they also wanted to cross over to Tibet just like the Dalai Lama did. It had always been his dream, just to see this magnificent city. Yangchen wrote back the same message: *We cross in spring, save money, and stay in touch.* Another person who lived in Kathmandu also wrote that going to Tibet was a lifelong dream.

Again, Yangchen sent the same message. Then she got to thinking: *It would be better if we all met up somewhere and traveled in a group.* She googled a map of Tibet, studying all the locations where the responders lived. Then she sent a message to the group:

'We need to meet as a group in Tibet. Some of you will need to leave sooner, like Dharmshala people, then us living in Nepal or Bhutan. I will send another message out soon as to where we can meet. If you have any suggestions, please let me know.'

She realized she needed to buy a map, as Lobsang suggested, and organized a trip down to Pokhara to buy one. Then she would be able to pinpoint exactly where to meet. The next day, she went to Pokhara via the one-hour bus ride and walked amongst the few tourists and locals in the rain to find a map. Many of the tourist shops were closed for the season, which frustrated her. She did find a store open and asked the store owner if he had a map of the region. He did not but pointed to a store down the street that might.

Yangchen went to the store, but it was closed for an hour. She decided to wait and went to a café for tea and momos. Having fresh cash with her was empowering. While drinking tea and eating her momos, she met a westerner who engaged her in conversation. He asked her if her ethnic roots were Tibetan. "Yes, of course. See my high cheekbones?" she said smiling as she smooshed her hands up emphasizing her cheekbones. He asked if she ever thought of going to Tibet.

"Of course!"

"You probably know you can go in a tourist group," he said.

"No, we can't," Yangchen correcting him. "Refugees have no status, no passport, and cannot go." The western guy's face took a muted expression. "And no money either," she added.

"How can you go?" he asked.

"We can't," she said glumly masking her plan.

Yangchen said goodbye as the hour was up and proceeded to the tourist store. It was open and she entered, walking straight to the counter where the shopkeeper stood.

"May I help you?" he asked.

"Yeah, do you have a map of Nepal and Tibet?"

"Yes," he said and pointed to a rack on the counter of maps.

"Oh!" Yangchen said half shouting. The shopkeeper took a map and handed it to Yangchen.

"May I?" she asked as she began to unfold the map on the counter to study it. The map was exactly what she needed and found all the crossing points for all the other people in the Tibet refugee group.

"Hmmm," she muttered to herself. "This will not be easy."

"Excuse me?" the shopkeeper asked. Yangchen lifted her head as she was so lost in her charting the course and forgot where she was.

"Oh, nothing," she said folding the map. "How much?"

CHAPTER THIRTEEN

AS THE MONSOON SEASON was in full swing, the days were long with having to stay inside most of the time. The family spent much of the time playing games like *bagh-chal* where one player controls four tigers and the other player controls twenty goats. Since only two can play at the same time, the winner takes on the next member of the family. Yangchen often won.

"You are too good at this game, my daughter," her father said. Yangchen was proud to have almost mastered the game, reinforcing her cleverness.

When it was time for sleep, often the rain would come down in buckets which caused for a restless sleep. There was genuine concern that if it rained too much, mud and floods could ruin their house. Everyone slept with one eye open when the heavy rain came.

June passed, July too, and then it was August. Soon Lobsang would return for high tourist season, to make as much money as possible to subsidize their trip. Yangchen had privately estimated the cost for supplies, cold weather gear and good walking shoes. She also knew to travel light and so they couldn't carry too much either. Planning would be strategic and precise and they couldn't do anything without a lot of money to spend. Plus, they would need money to stay in Lhasa. Returning home wasn't even in her budget, and despite the fact, she would most likely return to her family, she just wasn't sure how. But it also wasn't her priority.

Lobsang wrote to her that he would return late September. She made sure it was okay with her father, and he agreed keeping with his word. On the night before Lobsang was to arrive, she received a mysterious private message online. She didn't know who or even what exactly this person was. In his display picture, he had long hair, and his ethnicity seemed to be a blend of east and west. But it was his message that piqued her interest the most:

Tashi delek, I saw your Tibet post and crossing over. I would like to join your party when you cross. I have crossed before and can be your guide.

Yangchen thought long and hard about what he wrote. At first, she thought it would be a good idea to have a guide. But she was also concerned she had no idea who this person was. She decided to wait until Lobsang came and to discuss with him. She did write him back with only one question:

Who are you?

And then she put her phone down feeling a combination of curiosity and concern. She thought her next move would be to go with Lobsang back to the monastery and consult with her monk friend, Chen-tao.

When Lobsang arrived, Yangchen gave him a big hug, at the same time, practically dragging him by the collar to go to the monastery. On the way to the monastery, they shared an umbrella to shield them from the rain, Yangchen relayed this mysterious message to him.

"It is something we should consider, Yangchen," Lobsang advised. "I mean, do we really know where we are going?" Yangchen shook her head in a no.

"But I bought a map. I will show you later." He nodded.

When they arrived at the monastery, they repeated what they did last time to enter the main chamber and look for Chen-tao. It was always so hard to find him, so they made their presence known for him to find them. When the monks' prayers finished, Chen-tao approached them with the customary prayer hands to chest. Yangchen told the monk they had something to discuss with him. She told the monk about this mysterious message and asked if it is something that they should consider.

"Yes, young Yangchen, we should accept his offer," the monk said. "He can be a valuable resource." Lobsang asked if he was to charge money for his guide service.

"That is a good question," she said. "I will ask him."

They said goodbye for now to the monk and told him they would return soon with further information.

***

Yangchen was anxious to check her phone for any messages from this mystery person, but there were none. She wrote him back asking if he was charging them money. She set the phone down again. In the meantime, the monsoon began to fade away with less and less daily rain. Yangchen and Lobsang began their almost daily visits to Pokhara's Lakeside where the tourists congregated. Some days were profitable, other days little, if at all.

"We just need to stay consistent Yangchen, and soon we will have enough money."

One day, shortly after their first week of selling, Yangchen received another message from this person.

'*I will not charge you money. And as to who I am, I am a guide. And will be happy to be your guide too. I speak some Mandarin, Tibetan, some Nepalese and of course, English. We will meet in early spring.*'

When Yangchen and Lobsang read his message, they looked at each other and silently agreed he should be their guide. Yangchen wrote back immediately.

'*Of course, spring.*'

He responded immediately.

'*I will meet you in Pokhara. I will be back in touch early spring to arrange.*'

Yangchen and Lobsang were not only in agreement, but relieved and excited he join their little crusade.

Chapter Fourteen

THE FIRST THING YANGCHEN and Lobsang needed to do was to head back to the monastery to convey the good news to Chen-tao. When they arrived, he was out front minding the younger monks who were playing football in the front courtyard. He waved over to them as they approached.

"We have good news," Yangchen said excitedly. "This mysterious man said he would not charge to be our guide and wants to be our guide. He said he would come to Pokhara early spring."

"That is good news, good karma," Chen-tao said as he placed his hands to his chest.

"Yes," Yangchen said. "Now all we need to do is sell so many things to make money... and wait till spring."

The excitement died down for a moment as all three were deep in thought, evaluating what was needed for this journey. "I know we need good walking shoes, warm coats, food, all these things," Yangchen said.

"I have all these things," Chen-tao confirmed. "I will be ready."

"That is good," Yangchen said. "Lobsang and I go to Lakeside most days to sell Tibetan things tourists like to buy. We should have enough money before we leave to buy stuff."

Chen-tao smiled. "I am sure you are good salespeople. Not an easy way."

"No, it's not, but it serves our purpose," Yangchen responded.

"She is so good," Lobsang said. "She knows how to relate to the tourists, and they like her."

"We will come and visit you again with more news about this mystery man who will be our guide," she said.

"Does he have a name?" Chen-tao asked.

"Yes, just one name," she said. "His name is Bodhi." Chen-tao's eyes widened.

"Ah, he is an enlightened one," Chen-tao said. "Just like Buddha himself."

"It is good karma," Yangchen responded.

They said their goodbyes and walked back to Yangchen's home. When they arrived, her father was wearing a stern look on his face. "Yangchen," he said with concern. "What is this business with the monastery?" Lobsang looked over to Yangchen, and he spoke up.

"Just spiritual enlightenment, sir," Lobsang said.

"Hmmm," Dorje responded. "I suppose there is nothing wrong with that."

"It's good for me too, daddy. And I like my monk friend there." Her father nodded and went to sit by the eating area to pet Lucy. The other three kids joined in. Yangchen's mom was busy preparing dinner. Lobsang made a motion to Yangchen to step outside the house.

"What's going on, Lobsang?"

"Yangchen," he started. "You have not told your parents about this plan?" She shook her head in a no.

"Don't you think you should?" he asked.

"Well, yes," she started. "I don't like the idea of lying to them. That is not my way, and it is bad karma." Lobsang nodded his head. She continued.

"But I know, if I tell them, they will not let me go."

They remained silent, kicking at the dirt, deep in thought.

"I will think about it, we have some more time till spring," she responded. "If I do tell them, I would tell them we have a guide."

"I don't think that will calm them," Lobsang said. "They would be concerned about your safety. You know we would most likely be arrested and could remain in jail." Yangchen pondered on Lobsang's statement. "If we arrive in the night to Lhasa, they will never know we were foreigners and blend in. I will wear my *chuba* and look Tibetan."

"Maybe so."

"One thing I know," she began. "We need to go."

"I agree," Lobsang replied.

CHAPTER FIFTEEN

YANGCHEN CONTINUED TO MONITOR the Tibet refugee group online. Almost fifty different people from all over the region either said they would join in their movement, or pledged their support to go for it, and to let them know once she arrives in Lhasa. But most said they would go. Yangchen posted that they would have a guide to take them all the way to Lhasa. What she hadn't quite worked out yet was as to where they would all meet up somewhere in Tibet, particularly the people from Dharmshala as it is farthest away from the possible meeting point.

Yangchen studied the map when no one was home. She concluded that the small town of Shigatze in Tibet would be a good strategic place to meet and to camp way outside the town while waiting for the rest of the party. *But could they even find each other even then?* she wondered. She was consumed with important logistical details, and decided that if everyone weren't able to find each other, she would tell them they would simply meet in Lhasa.

***

The months ticked off the calendar, October, November, December, January. Lobsang would make periodic visits back home to be with his mom and return to Yangchen's home for more Lakeside selling. She would wear her *chuba* to look Tibetan as this was a proven attraction for tourists. It worked. By the end of January, they had enough money to purchase all that they would need for the journey and have enough money left over for expenses in Lhasa. Again, she contemplated her return to Nepal and if there would be any money left, but this just wasn't her concern. Getting there was.

February rolled around, and Yangchen wrote to Bodhi to set up a time for their meeting. She hadn't heard from him since they had first made contact months ago. And she hadn't heard from him for weeks after sending him a message. Then finally, she received a message.

I will meet you and your party at Lakeside, at the boat dock on March 1st, 10:00 AM.

Yangchen was excited and appreciated his conciseness. "10 AM," she repeated, "March 1st," to herself. Lobsang was back home. Yangchen sent Lobsang a message with the details of the meeting with Bodhi. He wrote her back saying he would come in the end of February and be there for the meeting. Yangchen also went to the monastery to tell Chen-tao to prepare for a bus ride down to Lakeside together early morning, March 1st. She also decided to tell her parents about her plans.

"I knew about your plan, Yangchen," her father said. "I found your map, and your constant selling trips to Lakeside made it easy to figure out." Yangchen's face flushed thinking she was in big trouble, her plans dashed.

"Your mother and I have privately discussed your venture," her dad said. "Many, many times." Yangchen stayed quiet and respectful. "It is so dangerous, so complicated, and we are very concerned about your well-being and safety."

"I know Papa," Yangchen said demoralized. Her eyes cast downwards. "It is a silly plan."

There was silence in the room. Yangchen perked up. "It's just," she started. "It's for grandfather." More silence pervaded throughout the house. Her brothers and sister and Lucy huddled in a corner. Her dad approached her.

"We know," her dad said softly. "He was a special man, and his karma believed you will successfully arrive in Lhasa." Yangchen smiled thinking of her grandfather. Yangchen's dad put both his hands on her shoulders.

"You have our blessings to go," he said. "Just be careful, of everything." She hugged her father and mother and bundled her brothers and sister together. It was a touching moment. And she was hugely relieved. "Such good karma," she said beaming and relieved.

CHAPTER SIXTEEN

OVER THE YEARS

SHORTLY AFTER THEIR ENGAGEMENT, Li and Tenzin were married in Beijing. Because Li's father was a high member of the Chinese Politburo, it was a grand wedding with Chinese culture of pomp and circumstance. Tenzin was nervous, as she was way out of her element, and didn't have anyone from Tibet to support her. But she loved Li and would endure whatever concern of estrangement that crept in and enjoy her wedding day.

Shortly after the wedding, the current supreme leader of China passed away. Li's father was in line to succeed him and became the Supreme Leader. Because of this, Li was being groomed to succeed his father and he enjoyed a career path of various appointments within the Politburo over the years. While Li spent much of his time serving the Party, Tenzin tended to their spacious home and met some other Tibetan women forming her own circle and support group. For the most part, she was happy living in Beijing. But often, she had a nagging and creeping feeling of homesickness for Tibet. This never went away.

Through time, Tenzin and Li had two children, a boy and a girl. Their combined ethnic blend of Han Chinese and Tibetan produced two lovely children. Li's family embraced Tenzin as their own and was thrilled she and her husband produced grandchildren. Li's father and mother were proud and delighted.

But Li's father suddenly died from a heart attack after serving the Party for only one year. At thirty-five, Li became the youngest supreme leader, the General Secretary of the Communist Party. Tenzin became the first lady.

Part Two

CHAPTER SEVENTEEN

THE APPOINTED DAY WAS finally here to meet with the mysterious Bodhi. Yangchen, her father, Lobsang and Chen-tao took the one-hour bus ride down by the boat dock at Lakeside Pokhara. They arrived early, and casually stood around on the lookout for this mysterious man.

It was 10 AM and there was no sighting yet. Yangchen paced up and back on the short pier. When she arrived at the end of the pier facing Phewa Lake, she quickly twirled around, and there he was with his long, greyish hair wearing a chuba. Yangchen quickly walked towards him, placing her hands to her chest.

"Tashi delek," she said. Bodhi bowed and pressed his hands together.

"Tashi delek," he said.

She looked at the other three members of her little party and proceeded to introduce them to Bodhi.

"I am happy your father is here," Bodhi said. He had no accent when he spoke, yet his appearance made him otherworldly. It was a contradictory contrast, Yangchen thought, which somewhat confused her and was interested to get to know his story.

"Come," Bodhi said. "There is my favorite tea café just over there. We can sit and talk about everything."

When they sat down, Bodhi ordered a big pot of tea for everyone and a couple of plates of momos. At first, everyone just kept to themselves, waiting for the tea to be served. When the tea arrived, Bodhi insisted he pour the tea into everyone's cup. He held his cup up as everyone followed.

"Bless this adventure, Lord Buddha." They took a sip, then another. The momos arrived and were set on the table. "Please," Bodhi said. "Enjoy. They make good momos."

Yangchen felt he was quite agreeable and friendly. Internally, the suspense of what he was about to say was building, yet she was waiting for him to take the lead. Bodhi popped a momo in his mouth and then another.

"Hmmmm, these are so good," he said. "Please, everyone, have more." The suspense continued to build.

"Okay, let's have this little meeting," he said. "First, each of you tell me a little about yourselves." Yangchen looked over to her father to start. "My dad's English is not so good, so I will translate." Yangchen said some words in Tibetan to her dad. Her dad took the last sip of his tea and spoke.

"He said, he is happy to meet you."

"Thank you, sir," Bodhi said. "I will lead a safe passage to Lhasa." Yangchen translated back to her dad. Dorje frowned a bit and said something in response to that. "He said, how can you be sure it will be safe?" Yangchen said.

Bodhi half-smiled, while nodding his head. "Because sir, I have crossed this way before and never had a problem." Dorje shook his head, and raised one more question, and spoke. "He asked why you cross this way. You can fly to Lhasa," she said.

"For the adventure, sir," Bodhi responded. "For the adventure. I have scaled many mountains in my time and have one more crossing before I hang up my climbing shoes."

Yangchen translated back to her dad, and he seemed satisfied, albeit somewhat skeptical, but approved of Bodhi to lead the journey. Dorje placed his hands to his chest for Bodhi, and Bodhi reciprocated in kind.

Bodhi turned to Yangchen. "Tell me Yangchen, what is your motivation for this trip?" He asked, and then cautioned. "It is not an easy expedition." Yangchen teared up a little. "It is for my grandfather," she started. "He was a High Lama in Lhasa and even knew Kundun."

"I see," Bodhi said, "I understand."

Yangchen continued. "He passed away last year and told me on his last day to go to Tibet." Yangchen tried to hold back her tears. "This journey is for him and all Tibetan refugees around the world." She breathed an emotional sigh and took a sip of her tea. Her hand shook a little from the sorrow.

"That is a bold statement," Bodhi reacted. "I will see you to Lhasa, Yangchen."

"And what about your two friends?" Lobsang spoke up.

"Yangchen and I are friends, since early school. I too want to go to Lhasa like Yangchen. My father passed away last year too, and he told me he wanted me to go to Tibet. It was his dying wish."

"I also understand, Lobsang. Welcome," he said placing his hands to his chest. Bodhi turned to Chen-tao. Chen-tao placed his hands to his chest and began to speak.

"I am a simple Buddhist monk. But my father is in prison in Lhasa, and I want to free him, take him with me back to Nepal." Bodhi simply pressed his hands to his chest. "You are welcome to join, my friend."

They all sat back in their chairs. Bodhi ordered another pot of tea for the table. They sat quietly in anticipation of what Bodhi had to say. The tea was brought to the table, and Bodhi poured another round for everyone. He held his cup up again. "And now, let me tell you my story."

"Yes, please, we want to know," Yangchen said excitedly.

"Okay," Bodhi started and took a breath. "You can see I am a hybrid of races and cultures, and I am." He tossed back his hair.

"My father is American, and my mother is Tibetan. They met in Lhasa a long time ago when foreigners could travel freely around Tibet. It was a grand and unlikely pairing, but it worked. They loved each other. My father arranged for a visa to the US after they were married in Tibet."

Bodhi stopped as if he were reflecting on his own story and took a sip of tea.

"I was born in the US, but half the time, we lived in Lhasa. I learned Tibetan language, and some Mandarin Chinese. I felt in my spirit I was more Tibetan, and this is how I live. My full name is Bodhi Karma Johnson." Yangchen smiled when she heard him say his name. "I am Bodhi to everyone."

Yangchen translated everything Bodhi said to her father. Bodhi spoke up again. "I am practicing Tibetan Buddhism." Dorje cleared his throat and asked a question with Yangchen translating. "He asked if you have a house in Lhasa where me and my friends can stay?"

"Yes sir, yes I do," Bodhi confirmed. "It is my family's home, and everyone is welcome to stay."

"Oh, that's great," Yangchen said. "I didn't know what to do, really, when we arrive there." Yangchen's dad cleared his throat again and spoke to Yangchen.

"He wants to know if you will lead us back to Nepal."

Bodhi's face went blank, and he thought what to say. "It is not my intention, sir. I want to stay a long time in Lhasa." Yangchen translated. Dorje's face was glum. Everyone was deep in thought. Bodhi started bobbing his head up and down.

"Okay," Bodhi started. "I will lead anyone back to Nepal when they want to return. I will make sure your daughter is safe, and everyone else." Bodhi stopped. "Yes, I will do this."

Yangchen translated back to her father, and he broke into a wide smile and placed his hands to his chest. Yangchen said, "You have his blessings for this journey." Bodhi reciprocated.

"Alright, the hard stuff out of the way, let's talk about this journey."

CHAPTER EIGHTEEN

"FIRST, THIS JOURNEY WILL be about a couple of weeks, maybe less. It depends on the weather and how quickly we can trek."

Yangchen looked over to Lobsang and Chen-tao, who had stayed mostly quiet during the conversation. Yangchen translated to her dad. He stayed quiet too.

"Yes, we are ready," Yangchen said.

"Good," Bodhi responded. "And everyone must stay healthy. Eating and drinking water is important." Yangchen nodded her head. And then she thought of something.

"Mr. Bodhi, sir," she started. "There is one thing."

"What is it?" Bodhi asked.

"You see," she started. "There are other people, like us, crossing when we do. I organized the movement online, and many people want to come."

"Yes, yes, I read those comments," Bodhi said. "That is how I found you." Yangchen thought for a minute. "You can lead them too?" she asked. Bodhi set back in his chair, deep in thought, putting his hand to his beard.

"You see, if there are too many people in one group, it will cause awareness by the Chinese army." Yangchen was sad because she had promised all the others from India, Nepal, Sikkim, Bhutan, they could come.

"I suggest we meet in Shigatze, on the western side of the town." Bodhi hesitated. "How many people are there?" he asked Yangchen.

"I don't know, maybe ten." She paused, then sheepishly added, "Maybe one hundred." Bodhi smiled.

"We will break up into small groups, waiting a day. There is a trail they can follow all the way to Lhasa." Yangchen nodded her head with relief. She did feel the responsibility for everyone as she was the organizer for this movement. They all sat back in their chairs.

"We will leave at midnight March 17; it is an auspicious day," he said.

"Why is it auspicious?" she asked while translating to her dad. Dorje spoke, as Yangchen translated. "My father says it is the day His Holiness left Lhasa for India."

"Yes!" Bodhi said excitedly. "It will be sixty years exactly on the midnight of the 17th, when Kundun left his sacred Potala Palace." A calm silence encased the table.

"One more thing: bring a heavy coat, some food you can eat, water, good walking shoes. But travel light. And your mobile will not work. There will be no communication." Yangchen looked at Lobsang with some intimidation. Bodhi being the spiritual being that he was, picked up on this.

"Not to worry, Yangchen," he reassured. "Safe arrival in Lhasa is my priority." He paused for a minute, then continued.

"Again, we will meet here at this boat dock at the stroke of midnight as the day turns to March 17." Pausing for a minute, he continued, "We will travel only at night. There will be a full moon to light the way."

They said goodbye, knowing that in sixteen days, their life would never be the same again.

CHAPTER NINETEEN

IN THE REMAINING COUPLE of weeks before their departure, Yangchen and Lobsang would head down to Pokhara to purchase the things they needed. Having earned the money required for this trip was a godsend. By the time they completed buying everything, there was still money left over for their stay in Lhasa. They bought good walking shoes, lightweight meals and snacks. And a heavy coat, gloves, a hat, and a backpack.

The rest of the time, Yangchen and Lobsang relaxed but took daily walks up and down the hills of Yangchen's village to stay in shape. They went to visit Chen-tao one last time to make sure he had what he needed. He said he did. They made final arrangements for everyone to meet at Yangchen's home. She said she would cover the taxi charge, as the bus didn't run that late. She said to be at her home at 10:30 PM on March 16th.

She also sent one more broadcast message to the Tibet refugee chat group:

I am leaving Pokhara on March 17th. We will all meet on the west side of Shigatze, but Dharmshala and other people need to leave ASAP as you have further to cross. If we don't meet in Shigatze, we will meet in Lhasa. Bon voyage!

Chapter nineteen

On the night of their departure, her father gathered the family around, and said prayers and blessings for their journey. Dorje gave Yangchen her grandfather's prayer wheel for good luck. She buried her head into her father's chest, looked up to him, and said "I love you, papa. Thank you for letting me go." She gave her mom, brothers, sister, and Lucy a good-bye hug. She grabbed her backpack, Lobsang doing the same, and left the house. Both the taxi and Chen-tao were standing by.

They took the drive down to Pokhara and walked the remaining thirty meters to the boat dock. Yangchen told the taxi driver to stay around, as she wasn't sure exactly where to go after the boat dock. That was Bodhi's responsibility. When they arrived at the dock, they couldn't see Bodhi. But there was a Buddhist monk sitting at the end of the dock, quietly reciting prayers. He was dressed in the customary yellow and orange robe. Yangchen thought that was curious at this time of night. She approached him as her footsteps on the wooden dock caused her new shoes to squeak. He turned around startling Yangchen.

"Ahh, here you are." It was Bodhi.

"But what happened to all your hair?"

"I shaved it. I am a Buddhist monk again," he said smiling.

Yangchen shook her head and smiled.

"Shall we go?" Bodhi asked.

"Yes, but where are we going?"

"Tibet."

"Well, sure, but from here?"

Bodhi pointed towards the direction of her village. Yangchen rolled her eyes.

"We just came from there...but I have a taxi to take us back." She led the way to the taxi that was fortunately waiting, considering how late it was in the night. They all piled into the taxi, bags and all, and pointed for the driver to take them up the hill.

Eventually, the taxi drove past her house. Yangchen enthusiastically pointed it out as the taxi drove on for another hour to an area she had not been before. Bodhi directed the taxi driver to an area where the light of the full moon allowed them to find the trail head. The taxi stopped, and they all got out of the car grabbing their bags. Yangchen looked towards the trail and straight up towards their first mountain pass. Bodhi noticed.

"There will be many high passes to cross," Bodhi said.

He took out a prayer wheel. Yangchen went digging into her pack for her prayer wheel and twirled it around too. Chen-tao also did, but Lobsang did not have one.

"Here," she said. "You can use mine." Lobsang twirled it around a few times.

"Okay, my friends," Bodhi said. "Let's go to Tibet."

They hoisted their backpacks on their backs and started their journey to Tibet.

"Here we go," Yangchen turned to Lobsang, murmuring under her breath.

CHAPTER TWENTY

THE CLIMB WAS ALREADY steep. Yangchen had to take periodic rests as she huffed and puffed her way up. Lobsang's pace was quicker, but he would always wait for Yangchen to catch up. Just ahead, Bodhi and Chen-tao were catching their own breath. Yangchen and Lobsang shared a rest with them. She put her pack down, sat on a tree stump, and let out an exhaustive sigh. Dawn was still hours away, but the light of the full moon assisted in guiding them.

"We have a long way to go," he said to Yangchen. She looked up at him.

"I know," she said. "Don't worry, I will be fine." Bodhi nodded his head.

"I rest a lot, but I will make," she said. "I have to."

Bodhi hoisted his pack and charged on. The rest of the party did the same. They had been walking in forested land, but eventually, the tree level gave way to more of a barren landscape. Big patches of snow dotted the landscape illuminated by the full moon. Bodhi was waiting for them at the base of the summit.

"This is our first la, pass," he explained and pointed to the summit where they would cross. "There are many to go, but once we reach the Tibetan plateau, it's a piece of cake." Yangchen smiled.

"That would be nice right now."

"What would be nice?" Bodhi asked.

"A piece of cake," she said half smiling.

"Haha...waiting for us in Lhasa," Bodhi said with a wink and motivation. "Onward."

The climb to the summit was slow. They were walking in snow now, sometimes half to one meter high. It took much effort, step after step. Yangchen took even more rests, almost after each step or two. Finally, the summit was in sight. From the moon's light, off in the distance, she could see Bodhi standing at the summit. Eventually, everyone caught up.

"Okay, let's do this," Yangchen said and plowed forward, not waiting for Bodhi.

Bodhi hustled up ahead of Yangchen. She smiled and shook her head, respecting Bodhi's leadership, and care. The grade was steep downhill. "Watch your steps, everyone," Bodhi cautioned. "Try not to step on any loose rocks after the snow."

Dawn's light began to slowly break, making it easier to see where they stepped. It was mid-morning by the time they reached the valley floor. Bodhi was way ahead and was sitting down. Yangchen could see that he had laid out a blanket to sit comfortably on. When they caught up, he said it was time for breakfast. Everyone had their own food. Yangchen's mom had prepared tsampa and Tibetan hard bread for the trip. She removed her pack and sat down to comb through taking inventory of her food before removing what she needed. Bodhi had brought along a little portable gas stove and had a tea kettle already boiling for tea. Everyone was quietly eating in between catching breaths from the climb they had just completed.

"We're making good time, people," Bodhi said. "I'm proud of you guys for keeping up." They felt good, and particularly Yangchen.

"You have done this trek before, from Pokhara?" she asked.

"Yes. A few times," Bodhi said. He poured tea for everyone, and they quietly sat sipping, while looking around at the beauty of their surroundings.

"This is still Nepal?" Chen-tao asked.

He pointed below on the other side to the next summit way off in the distance.

"Yes," Bodhi said. "You see the summit over there?" Bodhi asked. "And then there is another valley below, and the next *la* after that is Tibet." The reality of the long trek sunk in for Yangchen.

"That's when it becomes dangerous, yes?" Lobsang asked.

"Yes," Bodhi confirmed. "We will need to be on our toes."

It had been about an hour for their current rest. The sun was up but the morning air had a chill to it.

"It will be warm soon," Bodhi said. "Can we keep moving?" he asked.

"Yes, let's keep moving," Yangchen said.

"We can set up camp in a few hours, at the end of the valley before the next summit," Bodhi said. "As it is still Nepal, we can sleep at night." He paused. "But once we cross the border, it will be night trekking only."

"Yep, you already said," Yangchen said. Bodhi gave her an understanding look.

"I surely did, young Yangchen," he said. "You know, you remind me of my daughter: headstrong and determined and a bit sassy." Yangchen was surprised.

"Wait. You have a daughter?" she asked. "Where is she? Who is she?"

"With her mom, in the US," he said. "She is your age, too." He smiled with a sentimental look on his face. "I do love her so."

"Do you have a picture of her?" she asked.

"Yes," he responded. "I will show you later, but for now, let's move out."

"But Bodhi, why aren't you with your family, instead of us here?"

"I'll tell you later," he said adamantly. "Let's move." Yangchen just shook her head.

The valley floor was flat, with a periodic hill to climb. Yangchen was not too far behind Bodhi, with Lobsang and Chen-tao following behind Yangchen. She hustled up a bit to catch up to Bodhi and found herself walking beside him.

"Can you tell me about your daughter, Bodhi sir?" she asked.

"What would you like to know?" he asked. Yangchen thought for a minute, then her eyes brightened.

"Does she go to university?" she asked.

Just then, a pack of Nepalese yak herders walked towards them, replete with five big, burly, long-horned yaks. Bodhi moved to the side of the trail to let the yak herders pass them by. Bodhi said namaste, placing his hands to his chest, while Yangchen and the others did the same. The lead yak herder asked Bodhi a question. Although his Nepalese wasn't strong, he understood. He was asked if they were going to Tibet.

"Yes, we are," Bodhi answered. The man gave him a stern and concerned look. He responded to Bodhi's answer, but didn't quite understand. He turned to Yangchen, who understood and spoke fluent Nepalese.

"He said, to be careful, Chinese army on the other side."

"Tell him I am aware, and we will travel at night," Yangchen responded. The man spoke again.

"He said they have special army things, they can see at night."

"We will be careful," Yangchen responded to the yak herder.

The yak herder caravan moved on, the lead yak's cowbell tinkling as he swayed back and forth. Yangchen was deeply concerned. Bodhi did his best to allay her fears.

"Last time I made this trek, I had no problem," he said reassuring her. "I traveled at night, hid behind rocks during the day for sleep."

They continued their walk at a slow pace. Yangchen's mind was churning. Bodhi recognized her anxiety and knew exactly what she was thinking.

"Bodhi sir?" she asked "What will happen if the army finds us? What would happen?"

"We would be arrested," he said. "I can't sugar coat it, Yangchen." He paused as they continued their trek. "We just hope for the best, okay?" he stated. Yangchen nodded her head, but her spirits were stirred.

The party continued with their march and were quiet for the rest of the day. When it was about 4 PM, Yangchen had hit the wall from exhaustion as they had been walking since midnight. She fell behind. Bodhi saw there was a stream. "This is a suitable place to spend the night," Bodhi said. When everyone caught up, he said they would stay here, and to set up camp. Yangchen dropped her pack to the ground and quickly followed it, plopping herself down and let out a big groan.

"Oh my God, I am so tired."

Bodhi laid out the blanket. Yangchen crawled on to it, curling up in a fetal position and fell asleep. The other three worked around her, setting up tents and preparing *dalbhat* for dinner. Sometime later, Lobsang tapped her on her shoulder to wake her up to eat something. It took a while, but she finally lifted herself up to a sitting position. Lobsang handed her a bowl of *dalbhat* and spoon, and silently ate the entire bowl rather rapidly. Then she laid herself back down and was out for the night.

CHAPTER TWENTY-ONE

IT WAS DAWN WHEN Bodhi woke up and began to prepare tea. Chen-tao started to stir, then Lobsang. Yangchen was still out cold.

"I wonder if she will make it today?" Bodhi asked, looking over at the sleeping Yangchen. Lobsang shook his head. "She will," he said. "She is strong."

Everyone sat around sipping their tea and munching on tsampa. Yangchen finally started to move around, making yawning noises. When she opened her eyes, everyone was staring at her. She was their light, and all three felt such affection and admiration for her. And Yangchen? She was out of it.

"Mmmmffffpphh," she said groggily.

"Good morning to you, sleepy head," Bodhi said. "How are you feeling?"

"I don't know yet," she said yawning.

Yangchen sat up but with slumped over posture. She rubbed both her eyes. Lobsang poured her a cup of tea. "Oh," she said. "First, I need to take a trip to the forest. You know." She stood, cranked her neck from side to side, and walked about fifty meters into a forest of pines.

The other three debated a bit if they were to continue today.

"We are not in a hurry," Lobsang said, always protecting his friend.

"That is true, Lobsang," Bodhi said. "I am the guide, but Yangchen is our spiritual leader. We go at her pace."

Lobsang smiled. "Yes, she is."

Just then, they saw Yangchen running towards them, horror written on her face and screaming. The three quickly stood and ran towards her.

"What is it?" Bodhi asked.

"Come," she said squealing.

When they arrived, they immediately saw what upset Yangchen. A dead body. She covered her mouth with her hands. The body had been there for a while, all emaciated and half-eaten.

"He's wearing a *chuba*," Yangchen nervously exclaimed.

"Hard to know if he was coming from Tibet or going," Bodhi said. "But he is facing Tibet."

Bodhi circled in a little closer. "From the looks of things, he may have starved to death, and a long time ago." Bodhi backed away as an occasional fly buzzed around the dead man.

"Nothing we can do," Bodhi said. "Come on."

"Shouldn't we bury him? Yangchen asked. "Something?"

Bodhi thought for a moment. "No," he answered. "If any of his family is still looking for him, perhaps one day they will find him." Yangchen nodded her head in agreement. "Let's go back to camp," she said.

Bodhi whispered to Lobsang, "She is a leader, alright."

When they arrived back at their camp, Yangchen sat down. Lobsang poured her a hot cup of tea and handed her some of his tsampa. She devoured the tsampa and swiftly drank the tea. Handing her cup to Lobsang, she said, "More please."

They all quietly sat as the sun rose. Bodhi was hesitant to push. Yangchen stood up with her teacup in hand and looked towards the continuation of their trek. She saw a lofty summit ahead. "Wow," she said.

"Yes, it is a high summit," Bodhi confirmed. "In fact, it is one of the higher ones we will climb." Yangchen made a blowing sound, puffing up her cheeks. "I don't think I can do that today, guys."

"That is okay, Yangchen," Bodhi said. "We have all agreed we will go at your pace, okay?"

"Oh good," Yangchen said. "I am strong, but even I have my limits."

"How about this?" Bodhi asked. "We walk towards the summit as it is not too far. We camp the night near the base, and wake early to climb that summit?"

"Sure, we can do that," she said. They prepared to pack up their camp, and within a few minutes, continued their trek.

Their stride was slow after the previous day's long hike. Bodhi said it would only take half a day to arrive at the base of the summit. He continued to lead, with Yangchen following behind, and Chen-tao and Lobsang behind her. Yangchen quickened her pace to stride beside Bodhi. At first, no one said anything and focused on placing step after step on the trail, dodging rocks, and snakes as they went. Yangchen smiled at what she was about to ask Bodhi.

"Mr. Bodhi, sir?" Bodhi smiled.

"Please, just call me Bodhi. Everyone does."

"Okay, Bodhi." She shook her head as she wasn't used to calling strangers and foreigners by their given name without adding sir. "Bodhi, Bodhi," she repeated, smiling.

"Yes?" he asked.

"Umm, so do you know who Joan of Arc is?" she asked. He looked at her quizzically.

"Sure," he responded. "French girl from a long time ago who helped her people."

"Yes," she said excitedly. "You know her!" Bodhi nodded his head.

"Why?" he asked. "What about her?"

"She is my hero, and I pretend I am her. I am inspired by her," she said.

"But she was burned at the stake," he reminded her.

"Yes, you will see us through, so we don't get burned when we cross to Tibet," she cautioned.

"Don't you worry, Yangchen, I will do all I can for all of our safety." Yangchen's fear still wasn't alleviated.

"Are you sure?" she asked.

"Nothing in life is ever sure, Yangchen."

She allowed Bodhi to lead as she purposely fell behind. She stopped for a few minutes and took out her Joan of Arc book and flipped through a few pages. She was looking for the place in the story when Joan of Arc was most brave, when she defied the British. It worked for the moment until that time they tied her up to a wooden pyre and set it on fire.

"This time, it's gonna be different," she said defiantly. She then marched ahead passing Bodhi. "Your spirit knows no bounds, young Yangchen. You are the new Joan of Arc." She smiled and quickened her pace towards the base of the summit.

***

Chapter twenty-one

It was an uneventful walk to the summit accompanied by a pretty sunny day. Yangchen was ready to take rest. She wrestled with the notion that there was a long way to go. Her *polah*, grandfather, always told her when she did trek to Tibet, it would take some weeks. And it would be a chilling time ahead just setting foot in Tibet, not to mention walking through it. By the end of the day, she fell behind the other three. Lobsang always looked back towards her to ensure her safety. It was known that tigers and other beasts roam these forests of white oak and pine.

As the terrain flattened, Yangchen stopped for a sip of water. She could see Bodhi standing in one spot just ahead. She looked up and saw the towering snowcapped glistening mountains ahead. She shivered. When all four finally were together, Bodhi laid out the blanket. Yangchen plopped herself down, inhaling and exhaling some air. Bodhi looked over to her.

"You know, Yangchen, if you want to rest all day tomorrow, we can stay here," Bodhi said. "It's peaceful and still Nepal." Yangchen nodded her head, mostly in relief. She laid down horizontally for a few minutes and closed her eyes. But it wasn't long until she opened her eyes lazily staring up at the blue and orange sky. Sunset was upon them.

"Lobsang and Chen-tao, please gather some firewood," Bodhi asked. "I will make noodles tonight for good carbo-loading for tomorrow, if we go." Yangchen lifted her head.

"Carbo-loading?" she asked. Bodhi smiled.

"Yes, to load up on carbohydrates which convert to sugar which converts to energy," he said.

"Okay," she said and laid back down. This time she closed her eyes for a while and even fell asleep. Lobsang gently woke Yangchen. "Dinner time?" she asked.

"Yes, Joan of Arc," Bodhi said with a wink.

They calmly and quietly ate their meal. The screeching sound of an animal not too far away startled them. Bodhi stood and looked towards the direction of the sound.

"Tonight, we will take turns staying up and keep the fire going," Bodhi said. "We will all gather wood after dinner."

"What do you think it was?" Yangchen asked.

"I don't know," Bodhi said. "Maybe a tiger."

"Oh my God," Yangchen said dispiritedly. "What more?"

"Don't worry, they are usually afraid of people, and we will have a strong fire," Bodhi said. "Don't worry, Joan of Arc." She grimaced.

"Yes, she is my hero, but please call me Yangchen," she asked. Bodhi nodded his head with a guilty grin.

"Yangchen, Yangchen," Bodhi repeated while smiling.

CHAPTER TWENTY-TWO

BY THE TIME THEY woke up in the morning, there was an immediate sense of relief that no tigers had penetrated their camp. It was already a warm day. The group ate a quick breakfast, then swiftly packed.

"Ready to climb a mountain today?" Bodhi asked.

Everyone's reaction was one of quiet resignation. The previous few days of steady walking had already tired them out. "Okay, guys," Yangchen began trying to rally. "This is what we wanted to do, go to Tibet, right?" Everyone nodded in agreement. "So, let's go climb a mountain." She took the lead.

After a brisk two-hour walk, the group reached the bottom of the foothills of the lofty peak. Yangchen took a sip of water. She looked ahead, and saw it was nothing but a snowy and steep climb.

"Okay, let's do this," she said with determination. She forged ahead of even Bodhi walking with a quickened pace. She pulled about twenty-five meters ahead of Bodhi, as he accelerated his pace to catch up with her.

"Yangchen, you need to slow down a bit. It is already steep and going to get steeper," he cautioned. "In fact, it will take all day, maybe two before we reach the summit to the other side."

"Is the other side Tibet?" she asked.

"Yes, and you will need to change into your *chuba*," he said. "You know, to look the part."

Till now, she was wearing her athlete gear of black sweatpants and a t-shirt. Yangchen sighed a nervous sigh. Crossing into Tibet, of course, was the goal, but an intimidating one with the threat of the Chinese army everywhere. The last thing she would want is to be arrested and thrown into jail, and even though there was the potential of being tortured.

She let Bodhi take the lead, as he purposely slowed his pace and, in turn, would keep Yangchen's pace the same. Lobsang and Chen-tao followed her. As the day wore on, they would take periodic rest breaks. The foothills gradually gave way to the lofty snow-capped mountains that rose over eight thousand meters. When they reached the summit of the foothills, the wide-open Himalayan chain was in full view.

"You see those peaks?" Bodhi asked, pointing. "Once we cross to the other side and downhill, we will be near the border."

All four stood there for a while, to catch their breath and to conjecture on what they were about to attempt in the shadow of the incredible vista of the Himalayas. Yangchen removed her shoes and socks, sat down on the ground, and proceeded to give both her feet a massage. She noticed a blister on the back of her foot.

"Oh no," she cried. "Look."

Bodhi dug into his pack for a small first aid kit of some ointment and band-aid. He delicately took care of Yangchen's blister.

"You have a soft touch," she said.

"Thank you," Bodhi responded. "It used to be my job."

"To take care of blisters?" she asked.

"Among all kinds of things," he said. "I was a pediatrician a long time ago."

"Wow," Yangchen said. "Every time you talk about your life, you surprise me." Bodhi smiled.

"You will know all by the time we reach Lhasa."

"It was in US?" she asked. He nodded his head.

"Okay, put your socks and shoes back on, stand up, and tell me how that feels."

Yangchen stood, walked a few steps, and bounced up and down.

"Better?" Bodhi asked.

"Yes, better."

"Okay, let's move on," he said.

Having reached the summit of the foothills, their biggest ascent began. Initially, the ground was free of snow, but that was short-lived. When the steep climb began, snow was everywhere. The snow crunched under their feet, as it thaws during the day and freezes at night. This made the snow easier to walk on. Yangchen stopped for a moment to look towards what was ahead. Nothing but mountains that seemed to go on forever.

Bodhi walked back towards her.

"Are you okay?" he asked.

"Yes," she said. "Just looking ahead."

"It will be there waiting for us." They slowly trudged on. The morning gave way to the afternoon. Bodhi walked ahead of the three, as they were breathing heavily, stopping every few minutes. Bodhi was out of their sight, and they assumed he was just ahead. They reached the mini-summit towards the main summit, which loomed just ahead. Bodhi was sitting down and looking at the map Yangchen had brought along.

"Ah, there you are," Bodhi said cheerfully. "Come. Let me show you where we are."

Lobsang and Chen-tao crowded over Bodhi's shoulder. Yangchen gratefully sat down.

Bodhi put an X by one spot with a pen, and then a second X. He circled the first X.

"This is where we are now," he said. "And this second X is where we're going for the night."

"But is it still on this mountain?" Yangchen asked.

"Yes," Bodhi said affirmatively. "We will sleep on the mountain tonight." Bodhi stood up handing the map to Yangchen. Lobsang and Chen-tao sat next to her. They spoke softly amongst themselves as Bodhi walked a few meters. "Oh," he said, his voice resonating concern.

"Uhh, kiddos, we got to go," Bodhi said. "Storm is coming."

CHAPTER TWENTY-THREE

PRESENT DAY

FOR TENZIN, THE FIRST couple of years in Beijing were a time of resettlement and customization to the different culture and language. For the most part, this kept her busy. Eventually, she gave birth to a son and a daughter. As the years went by, Tenzin's life as the Chinese First Lady became more bittersweet. She did not enjoy the many public responsibilities she shared with her husband Li, the Supreme Leader of all of China. There were many state dinners and functions to attend with her husband.

It bothered her when she noticed the many strange and discomforting stares and behind-the-back comments because of her Tibetan ancestry. Not that the people of China disliked Tibetans. They simply viewed Tibetans as a curiosity. Yet, popular opinion was that their Supreme Leader was married to a Tibetan which disrupted the purity of Han culture. Those stares reminded Tenzin of her early days back in Lhasa with Li. Back then, she was content. Now she was uncomfortable, and this put a strain on their marriage. Since the birth of their children, her life and her marriage slowly turned her existence in China, meaningless. Tenzin's soul was slipping away.

In addition, two of her best Tibetan friends moved back to Tibet. She became increasingly homesick, lonely, and isolated. She loved her two children as they were the light of her life. But Li spent most of his time away from home running the country, often returning home late at night, or not at all. Their relation had soured. When Li was home, he would hole up in his study alone just to avoid the usual bickering about their life.

"You're hardly ever home," Tenzin said. "We're raising a family and I need you here at home more often. So do your children."

"But I cannot," Li said. "I am the Supreme Leader, which requires devotion and time to China." An awkward silence consumed them.

"And what about Tibetans?" she asked.

"What about them?" Li countered.

"Will you give them more autonomy and freedom from Chinese rule?" she pleaded.

Li shook his head.

"And what about Tibetan refugees?" she asked. "When can they return to Tibet?"

"They cannot," Li stated angrily.

"Upon our marriage, you had promised to help my people," Tenzin reminded him. "You have gone against your promise."

"Your people?" he shouted. "Always about your people. What about my people?"

He grumbled, as he turned the other way and left the room. His stubborn refusal was the turning point for Tenzin. She had concluded that Li had altered himself into something he was not back in Tibet.

"You have lost your soul," she said hopelessly. It was this that bothered Tenzin the most. She had fallen out of love, and this made her incredibly sad and angry.

* * *

It was Chinese New Year. For a week, Beijing was at its most festive, with firecrackers exploding everywhere. Long colorful and playful dragons streamed throughout the city as big drums set the soundtrack for a celebratory time.

Tenzin always enjoyed the new year time. Yet, this year she felt remorseful and sentimental as *Losar*, the Tibetan New Year coincided at the same time. As the Chinese First Lady, she would try to act like a First Lady, as these were her duties.

She and her husband and their two children would be chauffeured around and on to the Forbidden City to view the plaza safely and comfortably where the main attraction was to begin. When they arrived, they sat in the viewing balcony. Li commenced the festivities with a short speech of optimism for the citizens of Beijing and all of China. Tenzin flashed a Mona Lisa smile. She and her two children waved hello to the immense crowd below.

Tenzin always carried her phone inside her decorated purse. In the middle of the celebrations and merriment below, she could feel her phone vibrate. She looked over to her husband, separated by their two children. She discreetly pulled out her phone and found a message from one of her dear friends in Lhasa.

Tenzin dear, there is something important you should know. A friend of mine living in Dharmshala sent me a message that there are people crossing from Nepal towards Lhasa. My friend is part of an online Tibet refugee group, and she read a post from a Nepalese girl named Yangchen. She is the leader. She and her party are coming towards Tibet now. Please make sure they arrive safely.

Tenzin looked up and was startled. Her husband caught her with the phone in her hand and angrily motioned for her to put it away. She descended into deep thought while the celebrations continued. Her children squealed with excitement.

"Look mommy, dragons," shouted one of her children.

"Yes, pretty dragons," Tenzin said. The momentary distraction was brief, and she continued to form what she would tell her husband. She was immediately concerned for these brave people who were crossing over the treacherous and long journey back to Tibet.

* * *

When they arrived back to their palace, she requested the children's nanny Temina, to give them baths.

"I must speak with you," she said to Li in a hushed tone. They adjourned to their bedroom. Tenzin closed the door. They sat down at a table and chairs.

"Tell me," Li said. "What is it?" Tenzin had her phone in her hand. She pulled up the message and handed the phone to her husband. It took him a moment to read it and looked up at Tenzin. At first, he was silent. He looked at Tenzin squarely in the eye.

"I am aware of this," Li said. Tenzin was shocked and disheartened. "The army will arrest them."

This was Tenzin's breaking point. She was angry, displaying rare emotion.

"My husband," Tenzin said furiously. "Again. You promised to help free my people. These are my people."

"I cannot change such a rule as this," Li's voice rose.

"You are the Supreme Leader," she reprimanded and pleaded. "You can change anything."

CHAPTER TWENTY-FOUR

ONE LAST GASP OF winter carried the snow that roared in with a vengeance. The party of four put their heads down to safeguard themselves best they could from the driving snow as they slowly trudged ahead. But to where?

Bodhi was frantically trying to find some sort of snowdrift shield for the night. He stumbled upon one such place and shouted for everyone to come quickly. Before preparing their makeshift shelter for the night, he looked up to see if they were near any sheer point on the mountain for potential avalanches. Visibility was zero. He dug and dug, creating a larger snow drift, even to the point of creating a snow cave to keep them as warm as possible as their backs would be protected by the driving snow.

Yangchen, Lobsang and Chen-tao caught up with Bodhi and saw what he was doing. They all pitched in. The snow was heavier as the wind whistled, chilling them to the bone. The snowdrift that was to protect them was complete, and they all hunkered down sitting as close as possible to create some body warmth. The wind created such a noisy howl they could barely hear each other. But there wasn't much to say. Their only hope was to just survive the night. Bodhi had brought silver metallic thermal blankets to ward off the cold as much as possible.

As night fell, the heavy snowfall let up some. Bodhi stood and looked towards the peak for the potential for avalanches. It was still difficult to get a read, and now that it was night and it was getting colder. There was no way to make a fire, and they used every single piece of cover to keep them as warm as possible. Yangchen took out her pack to eat some tsampa. The others did the same, as they needed to eat and keep up their strength. Her hands shook from the cold.

"I am hoping this storm blows through, and at first light of morning, we will continue to get off this mountain," Bodhi said.

"We can make a fire to warm up at the bottom?" Yangchen asked.

"No," Bodhi said. "We will be near the border. A fire will alert the border guards."

It is not that Yangchen had second thoughts about this journey. It was for her *polah*. But the thought of finally crossing the border was an intimidating one. She shuddered from the thought and from the cold. She nuzzled closer to Lobsang and put her head on his shoulder. He put his arm around her for comfort and warmth. They fell asleep for a little while.

* * *

Dawn came and brought with it a deep orange sunrise. The four started to stir with Bodhi standing first. He could finally see the peak set against the orange sunrise sky. There were deep layers of snow, and the possibility of an avalanche was real.

"Come on, let's go," he said. "The summit's not far."

The four dusted the snow off themselves, grabbed their packs and laboriously climbed up and up. Each step was a major effort. Fresh snow was piled high, and it took all their efforts to place one foot ahead of the other. As the sun rose higher, blue sky emerged, giving them a boost of strength. Their breathing became more labored, gradually climbing further in elevation. They could see the summit with a towering peak of almost eight thousand meters. No one spoke to conserve energy.

Bodhi stopped just ahead to catch his breath and let the others catch up to him. He picked up a handful of fresh snow and popped it into his mouth. When Yangchen, Lobsang and Chen-tao caught up to Bodhi, he directed them to eat some snow to stay hydrated. With thin air and high altitude, the chance of dehydration amplified. They rested for a while, sitting down in the snow. They took out their food bags for some more tsampa, but not having much protein affected them, especially exerting so much energy. He took out his food bag and handed them each a protein bar. He took one for himself.

"This will get you to the other side," he said.

They unwrapped the bars, and vigorously and methodically chewed each bite, savoring the peanut and chocolate flavors, hoping for a burst of energy. Having eaten their bars, there was a sense of relief. Bodhi stood and looked towards where they were to go. Then he pointed ahead.

"You see the peak?" Bodhi asked. "Just to the right is the *la*, the pass. That is where we will go next."

"It doesn't look so far," Yangchen said.

"It's not," Bodhi said. "We can do this."

The other three gradually stood in unison and struggled to hoist their packs once again, and slowly trudged on. The morning gave way to the afternoon. With each pain-staking step, they were closer to where they wanted to be. Exhaustion was setting in. Chen-tao said he had a headache, indicative of altitude sickness. Bodhi had him sit down to rest. The others took advantage and did the same. Bodhi removed his pack and dug deep inside, removing most of what was in there. He pulled out a small metal cylinder and a mouth mask and turned the small nozzle and handed the mask to Chen-tao.

"Oxygen," he said. "Breathe deep and slow."

Chen-tao followed orders and did just that. He once removed the mask to breathe naturally, then placed it back over his mouth. A few minutes went by, and then he removed the mask altogether.

"How you feel now, Chen-tao?" Yangchen asked. Chen-tao nodded his head.

"Better...yes," Chen-tao said. "Headache finished."

"Good," said Bodhi. Chen-tao handed Bodhi the tank and mask. "Eat some snow," Bodhi advised Chen-tao. "Stay hydrated."

Yangchen looked at him curiously, shaking her head and smiling.

"What else do you have in your pack?" she asked.

"Only important lifesaving things, Yangchen," he said.

"You are a good guide, Bodhi," she said.

"OK. Onward?" he asked.

They all stood and trekked on, but the end was in sight.

CHAPTER TWENTY-FIVE

IT TOOK THE LAST of their energy and most of the afternoon, but they finally reached the summit's pass. Bodhi, of course, reached the top first. The other three were far behind. He whistled to them and waved his arms, flashing a wide smile. Yangchen led the other two.

"Come on, guys," she said, "We're almost there."

When they arrived to where Bodhi was, they all stood looking down on the other side. They had the snowy peak to descend, but there was relief at the prospect there weren't any huge peaks to climb next. Bodhi pointed to the horizon.

"Tibet," he exclaimed.

"Really?" Yangchen said.

"Yes. The Tibetan plateau is ahead."

The snowy mountain gave way to dry land towards the bottom where spring had already arrived. All four sat down to catch their breath.

"Let's just rest here for a while," Bodhi said.

They all sat there quietly, resting. The heavy respiration of climbing this huge mountain began to settle down. They all dug into their food stash and munched on tsampa washed down with a handful of snow. Bodhi was unusually quiet, lost in thought. Yangchen was staring a hole right through him.

"Wow," he said under his breath.

"Wow?" Yangchen said. "What is it?" He looked at her with wet eyes. She was confused.

"Tibet," Bodhi said reflectively. "I first crossed here in 1985, when independent travelers could travel around Tibet, no problem." Yangchen simply blinked, not sure where Bodhi was going. The other two were listening intently.

"Why are you crying?" Yangchen asked. Bodhi looked at her and slightly smiled.

"Do you know what the first guy to climb Mt. Everest said?"

"He said because it's there," Lobsang piped in. "And it was Edmund Hillary from New Zealand."

"That's exactly right, Lobsang," Bodhi confirmed. "Because it's there."

"And you crossed because it is here?"

"Yes," Bodhi said. Yangchen looked at him foolishly.

"You crazy, man," she said, laughing. Then the other three joined in the laughter.

The laughter settled down, and Bodhi was reflective again, as they continued to stare down and off to the horizon to what was waiting for them.

"The thing is, my friends," Bodhi began, "Adventure and doing crazy things are in my DNA. I just have to."

The other three remained quiet knowing that there had to be more to this story. They waited patiently for anything to come next from Bodhi, but it didn't come. Yangchen being the persistent and inquisitive one, kept it going.

"Okay, crazy Bodhi. Please tell us your story so we don't need to ask you any more questions," she requested. He looked at her with affection and shook his head.

"You and my daughter would get along so well," he said.

"Why?" Yangchen asked.

"Because you both have the same impetuous energetic qualities, always asking questions, and both very smart…and very nosy."

"Well, I want to meet her," she said.

"I hope you get to," he said.

"Okay, here is my story," Bodhi started. "As you know, my dad met my mom in Tibet. He was a doctor on loan to a hospital in Lhasa, training other doctors and nurses. That is where he met my mom, as she was a nurse there. A Tibetan nurse."

Yangchen and the others sat spellbound listening to Bodhi's story.

"Finally, they moved back to the US, and were married in Tibet and the US, and then they had me."

"That's it?" Yangchen asked. Bodhi looked at her with kindness as he appreciated her keen interest.

"Well, okay," he resigned to continue. "I went to medical school, graduated and practiced as a pediatrician at a big hospital in New York where my dad was from." Bodhi paused, reflecting on his own life story.

"And then?" Yangchen asked.

"And then I met my wife, she was a nurse at the hospital, we fell in love and got married," Bodhi relayed.

"And then?" Yangchen asked.

"And then we had Sara Chodren, our daughter," Bodhi stated. Yangchen wasn't quite satisfied.

"Where are they now, your wife and daughter?" Yangchen asked.

"In New York," Bodhi answered. "And now we need to go."

The sun was starting to set, and they had a long way to go all downhill.

"Do you have energy to make it to dry land?" Bodhi asked. The other three looked at each other, questioning Bodhi's request with their facial expressions and body language.

"No," Yangchen said. "But let's go anyways." Bodhi gave them each another protein bar and they hungrily devoured it.

"To the bottom," he exclaimed. Once again, they hoisted their packs and practically skipped down the mountain. Yangchen fell a few times and rolled down the mountain some meters, then stopped, giggling all the way. The others ran up to her, but she was alright and was still giggling.

"This is kinda fun," she said.

"But there are rocks covered in all this snow," Bodhi cautioned. "So be careful."

She picked herself up, dusting the snow off, and slowly and steadily marched down the mountain. It was now dark, and the waning moon barely lit the slope. But they could tell they were making progress and dry land was in sight.

"We can camp at the bottom as it is still Nepal," Bodhi said. "And rest for a day or two...the hardest part will be over."

The rest of the way they traveled as if they were on autopilot. They were numb, they were exhausted, but dry land was a massive incentive to keep going. They would periodically take short rests and keep moving. It was nearly dawn when they touched dry land. When they did, they all fell to the ground, lying flat on their backs. Nobody moved and didn't speak for a couple of hours. When they did wake, it was dawn again.

"Come," Bodhi said. "There is a rock cropping over there, and we need to stay behind it. This is still Nepal, but the border is not too far away."

Realizing they were about to cross the border sent an inevitable chill through Yangchen and she forgot all about being happy.

CHAPTER TWENTY-SIX

EVER SINCE TENZIN LEARNED of the crossing by Yangchen and her party to Tibet, she was nervous, anxious, and concerned for their safety. But most of all, she was disappointed by her husband Li. He had the power to protect them when they crossed into Tibet but had done nothing to ensure their safety. As he knew of Yangchen and the party's crossing, she assumed he had alerted his army. She went to confront him.

"Will you allow them to cross safely?" she pleaded with him in one more attempt.

"It is how things are, and their fate is out of my hands," he said. Tenzin was practically in tears.

"You are not my dear husband anymore," Tenzin began. "How you have changed since becoming the Supreme Leader!" He looked at her mournfully but remained steadfast in his own convictions. "Why have you become to be this way?" Li remained silent. She made a smack sound in disgust. Tenzin knew what she needed to do.

She spun around and left the room determined to take matters into her own hands. Temina, their nanny and Tenzin's confidant was playing with the children. Temina heard the raised voices and felt extreme tension between the estranged couple. She closed the door behind her and went to sit by them.

"My dear children," she started. "I love you so much." They looked at her with love, while continuing to play with their toys.

"We are going on a journey," she told them.

"Where mama?" asked her five-year-old son. She whispered. "Somewhere you have never been," she said mysteriously while desperately trying to hold back her tears.

"Is daddy coming with us?" asked her four-year-old daughter. Tenzin shook her head. They frowned for a moment, but their toys distracted them from their mom's vital message.

"Let's pack your bags, and only take important things," Tenzin said. "I will help you." She turned to Temina. "You are coming too. Go pack your bag," she advised Temina.

Tenzin removed two small suitcases from their closet and hastily packed clothes and toys and their toothbrushes in their bags. Li shouted through the door that he was leaving the house for a while to attend a meeting at the Politburo.

"Good," she said to herself. She heard the front door close, went to her room to pack a bag and staged all four bags by the front door. She wrapped a scarf around her head to be inconspicuous and left a very brief handwritten note by the door.

"We have gone to Tibet."

***

The streets were always crowded, which helped to remain inconspicuous. Eventually, Tenzin hailed a taxi to the massive train station. Temina bought four tickets for the three-day train ride to Lhasa. Tenzin swore her to secrecy not to say anything to anyone.

The station was busy, and Tenzin was a little confused about where to board their train. She focused on the big schedule board that was always flipping its characters for when any train were to leave and which platform. She saw the platform to Lhasa and held her two children's hands as they rolled their suitcases towards the train. She showed the conductor her tickets and he led them to their compartment, that she insisted be private just for her and companions.

They put their suitcases away and sat back and relaxed, knowing this was to be a long journey. Tenzin let out a deep sigh. Her children sensed her anxiety. Her son especially was sensitive to the situation and that their dad was not with them.

"Mommy?" he asked. "Is daddy going to join us?"

"Daddy is very busy, my son," she said. "But he may come. We will be there for a while."

Her son stayed quiet. The train began to move out of the station slowly.

"This is good," she said. "We can relax now. I ordered dinner to come to our compartment." They were preoccupied looking out the window as the station gave way to the night.

CHAPTER TWENTY-SEVEN

THE FOUR WERE COMPLETELY exhausted and rested all day. They had literally climbed and descended a mountain. Their clothes were wet and one at a time, each went behind a large boulder to change into dry clothes, then spread out the wet clothes to dry in the hot sun. Bodhi brought out his mini stove and made *dalbhat*, lentils and rice, rich in protein and most welcome by all.

Once in dry clothes, they gathered around, feeling safe and out of harm's way and were ready for Bodhi's special *dalbhat*.

"I added extra chili pepper," Bodhi said. "Gives it a kick."

Everyone was unusually quiet, lost in their own thoughts. Yangchen's concern of crossing the border was running high. She was about to speak but thought better not to now and to allow everyone to finish their meal. The warm afternoon gradually gave way to a chillier evening. Their clothes had all dried, and Yangchen went to change back into her athlete's gear. Bodhi was looking at her as she approached the minicamp.

"You know, Yangchen," Bodhi said. "When we leave camp tomorrow, you will need to be wearing your *chuba*. You too, Lobsang. We need to look as ordinary as possible all the way to Lhasa."

"I know," she said.

"By the way," Bodhi said. "We will rest here tomorrow too. Tomorrow night when it is pitch black out, is when we will cross the border."

***

After an uneventful and restful night, dawn broke. Bodhi was up first and boiled some water for tea. He brought out the last of the hard-Tibetan bread. He was hoping to meet other pilgrims and travelers along the way, so they could buy some food from them.

The day was more for rest as well as waiting for night. They ate more *dalbhat* as their strength had returned, and all were gearing up for the next part of their journey. Much of the day was spent in contemplative silence, knowing the party was to cross the border that night. Yangchen noticed that Bodhi was particularly and unusually quiet. She cleared her throat to say something, anything, but thought not to. Shortly a bit later as they continued to sit around and rest, Bodhi cleared his throat.

"The thing is, guys," he said, "this trek is not for adventure. I have a purpose too, just as you three do."

"Tell us, Bodhi," Yangchen said as she was engrossed with what he was about to say and moved closer to him.

"You see, my mom is sick, and I am bringing her medicine," he spoke as he touched his pack. "She is in Lhasa." Yangchen blinked a couple of times.

"But why don't you fly there, or she fly to America for medical care?" she asked.

"Yangchen, the truth of it is, I can't go to Tibet, legally," he declared.

"Why not?" she asked.

"Because they kicked me out, permanently," he said. There was a long pause, as Bodhi let out a huge sigh. "It's because of the 2008 Tibet uprising. I helped to start the movement, and they found out, arrested me and then permanently expelled me from the country and never to return." He paused for a few minutes. "Until now."

"But why can't your mom fly to America for medical care?" Yangchen asked.

"They took away her American passport," he answered. "My dad had passed away a few years before, and my mom returned home. I have not seen her since 2008, and now she is sick." Another long stretch of silence as Bodhi reflected on his final declaration. "If I enter Tibet, they will arrest me." Yangchen gasped. "Then we would be arrested," Yangchen became uncharacteristically upset.

"Why didn't you tell us that back in Pokhara?" she asked mournfully.

"Yangchen, I saw how determined and eager you were to go," Bodhi responded. "If I did tell you, we wouldn't be here now. Right?"

Chen-tao, in a rare moment, started to speak to diffuse what had become an awkward moment.

"We all have good purpose to go to Tibet," he started. "All four of us united for the same cause."

He clasped his hands together in prayer fashion and began to softly chant a Buddhist prayer for a safe journey. "We will make a safe journey."

Early evening had fallen. Lobsang and Yangchen were off by themselves a few meters away from the main camp. Bodhi approached them.

"Put on your *chubas*, you two," he said with authority. "It's time to cross."

CHAPTER TWENTY-EIGHT

THE PARTY OF FOUR left their camp, and eventually Nepal, behind. The border was close. Even though it was night, discretion was paramount. Bodhi told the three to wait and stay quiet as he approached the border. He could see lights from a not too far off camp, most likely Chinese soldiers. He walked parallel to the border, still staying on the Nepal side. The lights in the distance disappeared behind a hilly rise that separated the border. Bodhi went back to where Yangchen, Lobsang and Chen-tao were apprehensively waiting.

"Come," he said. "Follow me closely, and stay quiet, please."

Bodhi found where he was just a bit earlier, about a two-hundred-meter walk.

"Okay," he said. "Let's cross."

And so, they did. At first, they were nervous and whatever calmness they felt while in Nepal was gone. But at least the walk was flat, with only a few rises here and there. Bodhi stopped for a minute and took out a compass to give him the proper direction towards Shigatze where they were to meet Yangchen's online fellow refugees. As the compass was illuminated, Bodhi could decipher that they were heading in the right direction. The four walked through the night.

Fortunately, it was uneventful as the only lights from anyone were near the border, and they were now well within Tibet, walking over the plateau. Dawn was nearing, and they had to search for a safe place to conceal themselves during the day and try to get some sleep. But the plateau was mostly flat and rocky with no trees or forests to hide in.

There was a slight rise, and Bodhi felt it was good enough to camp behind during the day. All were tired and relieved to stop for the next fourteen hours until night fell again. As light broke, they could clearly see that the landscape was flat. A stark contrast to the mountains and forests of Nepal. When they spoke, it was brief.

"Bodhi? How far is Shigatze?" Yangchen asked.

"A couple of days or so, walking just like this," he answered.

Silence and apprehension consumed them as the sun gradually rose into the sky. He gathered everyone in a tight circle.

"Listen," he started. "If any soldiers approach us, how we all look appears we are blending in. But if they ask for papers or identification, pretend you don't know Chinese language."

"That's easy," Yangchen said smiling. "Because I don't know it."

"Just hope they don't ask for ID," he said.

Bodhi reached into his pack and brought out four wooden hand-sized blocks. Yangchen nodded her head. "I know what those are for. For prostrations," she said.

"Yes," Bodhi said. "You will look the part doing this in case we see soldiers approaching us."

They stayed vigilant throughout the day, taking turns to sleep, and waited for nightfall once again.

CHAPTER TWENTY-NINE

THE THREE-DAY TRAIN RIDE to Lhasa was long and tedious. Most of the time, Tenzin was worried that she would be recognized when they arrived. She was aware of her countrywide visibility, but maybe in Lhasa, she would be more anonymous. When the train arrived into Lhasa's train station, she and her two children remained behind until the train emptied. Looking outside, Tenzin could see the crowd from the train had dispersed. She covered her head with her scarf, and placed two baseball caps on her children, adjusting the caps as low as possible on their heads and leaving just enough to see in front of them. They left the train.

Fortunately, they were not bothered and caught a taxi to a tourist hotel. The taxi dropped them off, and Tenzin escorted her kids and Temina. She had Temina check in with her passport to maintain her anonymity and they were shown their room. With the door shut, Tenzin and the children laid down on their bed, totally exhausted. She spoke with her children.

"Tomorrow, you will stay in the room with Temina, as I have some business to attend to, and then I will return for lunch, okay? In the meantime, here is the TV remote and you can watch some TV."

"Okay mommy," they obediently said.

***

The next morning, Tenzin securely wrapped her scarf around her head and put on a *chuba* and left the room. Tibetan women typically and proudly show off their long hair uncovered, and Tenzin was concerned wearing her scarf may lead to suspicion and discovery. But she also thought she would be easily recognized without it.

She walked swiftly to where her friend lived, the same friend who had sent her a message about the group from Nepal who was crossing through Tibet. Tenzin had sent her a message prior to leaving Beijing that she was coming and hoped her friend would be home. When she knocked on her door, her friend Sangye answered.

"Tenzin dear, you look wonderful," Sangye said. "Please come in." Tenzin looked both ways before entering allaying for any suspicion. They gave each other a warm, tender hug. Sangye directed her to have a seat, while her friend went to prepare tea. It was a minute when Sangye brought a pot of tea and Tibetan bread. She sat down and poured two cups of tea.

"So, how are the kids?" Sangye asked. Tenzin thought a minute before answering.

"They are good," she said. "But also confused why their daddy isn't with us." Sangye mused on that comment. Tenzin kept the dilemma of her marriage secret to all, except for her caretaker Temina.

"Why is he not here?" Sangye asked perplexed.

"Oh Sangye," Tenzin woefully bemoaned. "Things are not good."

"But why?" she asked. "You two used to be so in love ten years ago." Tenzin shook her head.

"Not anymore," Tenzin said downwardly. "The responsibility of Supreme has crippled our marriage." Tenzin wept a bit. "He has changed."

"I understand," Sangye said. They fell into silence, sipping their tea and taking a couple of bites of the fresh Tibetan bread. Sangye politely gave time and space for her dear friend Tenzin. Tenzin looked up at her with dampened eyes. Sangye handed her some tissues, as Tenzin dabbed her eyes.

"Being the First Lady, even though is important for China, it is not important for me," Tenzin said. "Sangye, I am Tibetan, first and foremost, and I always will be."

Sangye nodded her head in agreement.

"Let me remind you of a story," Tenzin began. "When Li proposed to me, I asked him to help with the situation of Tibetan people, and he agreed."

"Yes, I remember. You told me that ten years ago," Sangye said.

"Well, he has done nothing," Tenzin said. "Ever since the 2008 uprising, people here are watched over, questioned, scrutinized, sometimes beaten or thrown in jail...and some just disappear." Tenzin asked for more tissues to dry her eyes. Sangye poured her a second cup of tea.

"When you sent me the message about the people from Nepal crossing to Lhasa, that sent a tremor right through me," Tenzin said. "And I felt the need to help them, and to ensure their safety, just as you suggested. Knowing my husband would not help, I came here to Lhasa to see what I can do." Sangye put her cup down and took Tenzin's hands into hers.

"Tenzin dear, it isn't just this party from Nepal," Sangye said. "It's people from all over. Dharmshala, Sikkim, Kathmandu, Bhutan. All crossing."

"Oh my God." Tenzin took her hands and covered her mouth in surprise of the realization. "It's a reverse migration back to Tibet!"

"Yes," Sangye said. "Tibetan refugee people are coming home, and they are all meeting in Shigatze to march to Lhasa." Tenzin took a few sips of tea, thinking of what she had just learned. Her eyes brightened.

"We must go to Shigatze and meet them, and escort them safely to Lhasa," Tenzin said defiantly. "However, I am sure my husband will have his army there."

"How can we go there?" Sangye asked.

"Can you arrange a trustful driver, a friend?" Tenzin asked.

"Yes, my cousin," Sangye said. "He has a taxi. He is ready any time."

"Good. We travel tonight."

Chapter Thirty

NIGHT FELL, AND WITH only a spoonful of *dalbhat*, the group picked themselves up, and continued their nightly crusade across the Tibetan plateau. Bodhi ordered them to stay quiet, and march in single file, keeping about twenty meters of space between, not to arouse suspicion. They did just that for most of the night without any incident. Off in the distance, Bodhi saw the bright headlights of an oncoming vehicle quickly heading towards them.

"Lobsang, Yangchen, get out your prostration blocks, and when I say begin, start your prostrations. You know what to do." The lights grew closer. "Okay, now.

Lobsang immediately followed suit, and Yangchen had to observe him to know what to do.

"This is hard," she said, exerting all her energy as they both slithered parallel to the ground, kneeled on two knees and then stood straight up, clapping the two wooden blocks together. They repeated these actions every two steps, again and again. "I don't know how people do this," she whispered.

"Shhhh," Bodhi said. "They're almost here."

The vehicle arrived and slammed on the breaks just in front of the party creating a cloud of dust. Dawn was breaking. They could see the British green color of a jeep with the Chinese flag waving in the back. The party stopped in their tracks. Yangchen and Lobsang stayed parallel to the ground, their heads buried in their arms in front of them.

Two Chinese soldiers left the vehicle and said something in Chinese to the party. Bodhi could not quite understand what they said. But their tone was hostile. They pointed their rifles towards Yangchen and Lobsang, signaling them to stand. They kept the wood blocks in their hands. Yangchen was shaking and tried to conceal it.

Bodhi spoke to them in Tibetan, but the soldiers did not understand. One of the soldiers pointed his rifle at Bodhi. Bodhi put his hands out to show the soldiers he was not armed. The other soldier put his hand out to appear, he was asking for something. Bodhi made a gesture he didn't have what they wanted: identification. With one soldier continuing to point his rifle at the party, the other soldier starting rummaging through each person's pack. When the soldier found Bodhi's oxygen tank and mask, the soldier jumped back, uttering a growling sound. Then he took his rifle, and both soldiers remained vigilant with their standoff. Bodhi made a gesture of full and extended hand to mouth and gestured over to Chen-tao. The two soldiers approached Chen-tao and looked him over.

Chen-tao stood like a statue then clasped his two hands together in prayer fashion. He started to say a prayer, but one of the soldiers barked to silence him. Chen-tao stopped. They moved towards Yangchen and Lobsang and searched their packs as well. One solider removed Yangchen's Joan of Arc book and clearly saw that the book was not written in Chinese. At first, she was frozen, but then she summoned up all her courage, and grabbed the book back from the soldier. He jumped back and pointed his rifle with hostility and intent. Bodhi made hand gestures asking if they could continue.

The two soldiers moved back to their jeep and radioed. The party heard a crackling noise on the other end to whomever the soldiers were talking to. The communications soldier hung up, and both soldiers moved back to the party. "Lhasa," Bodhi said mustering up the best of his Tibetan accent.

The two soldiers kept their rifles pointed towards the party of four as they walked backward to their jeep. They entered and sped off, leaving another cloud of dust in their wake. They stayed silent while standing steadfast until the jeep disappeared over the horizon.

"Oh my God," Yangchen said with a shaky voice. "I've never been so scared in my life."

They all let out a collective breath.

"But Bodhi, why didn't they arrest us?" Yangchen asked.

"I overheard that they were required to go to Shigatze," Bodhi said. "Maybe your other refugees are there now." Yangchen grimaced at the thought that they were in trouble and shook realizing their predicament had become very real.

***

The sun started to rise, as Bodhi, ever the absolute guide, looked in all directions to find a hill, or a rise for safety and to spend the day out of the sun. There was a rise off in the distance, and he directed the party to walk that way. They stayed silent the entire time. Arriving at the new day camp, due to their exhaustion and fear, they collapsed to the ground.

"We need food," Bodhi stated. He crouched at the top of the rise on the lookout for any pilgrims and passersby for the possibility of buying or exchanging something for food. No one was in sight. The sun began to set. Bodhi came back to the other three below the rise to search his pack for any remaining food. He found a protein bar at the bottom of his pack and divided it into four equal parts. He asked the others what they were left with, which all three had gone through the rest of their food too. Bodhi grew genuinely concerned. Their water was minimal too, as they had filled their bottles with snow just before entering dry land.

"We are two days away from Shigatze, people," Bodhi said. "Somehow, we just have to make the rest of this trip on will power and adrenaline...or get really lucky and find some people." He tried to stay buoyant. "A small bite of protein bar is just going to have to do." Yangchen perked up.

"My friends," she started. "We came on this trek with a mission, and this mission isn't going to fail us. Mind over matter is especially important. If you feel hungry, do not think about it. Think about a nice meal in Lhasa when we get there."

They all nodded their heads in agreement. It was now nightfall and time to move on. The faster they walked, the quicker they would arrive in Shigatze and be able to get food and water.

CHAPTER THIRTY-ONE

TENZIN'S MOBILE VIBRATED, ALARMING her. It was a text from Sangye announcing she and her cousin had arrived at the hotel.

"Okay my dear children, mommy must go now to meet some people coming from Nepal. They have walked a long way, and they must be tired," Tenzin explained to her children. "Where is Nepal, my mommy?" her son asked. "Very far away." She tried to fight back tears.

"Temina will take good care of you until I come back, okay?" The children became a bit agitated and concerned that their dad and now their mom were abandoning them. Tenzin comforted them as best as she could, but also knew they were in good hands with Temina. Of course, Tenzin had no idea where Yangchen and the others were at this moment in their journey. But she wanted to arrive before they did. It was exceedingly complicated to leave her children behind, but she was resolute for her cause. She kissed them each goodbye.

It was the dead of night when the taxi drove Tenzin and Sangye towards Shigatze, about a five-hour drive. Dawn had not broken yet and as the taxi approached the small town, Tenzin asked the driver to turn his lights off to alleviate any suspicion of their mission. "Keep driving past town, to the west side," Tenzin requested.

The taxi arrived on the western fringes on the other side. It was still very dark out. "Just keep driving slowly," Tenzin said. It was more than a couple of kilometers away from Shigatze.

"Ohhh!" Tenzin exclaimed. "Look. There are lights. Go that way instead, away from the army camp."

The taxi went another couple of kilometers. "Let's just park here for now," Tenzin said, "until light."

An anxious hour went by and finally a crack of light started to appear.

"Let us go now," Tenzin said to the driver. Sangye turned to Tenzin.

"Tenzin, we are not sure anybody we are looking for are here," Sangye stated.

"That may be true, Sangye," Tenzin said. "And I thought of that too." Tenzin thought for a moment. "Driver, please move on, that way" Tenzin said as she pointed. "Slowly." She turned to Sangye and took her hand. "I am feeling that people are here," Tenzin said. "Somewhere out here."

They drove on for a bit. Suddenly the driver pointed. "Madame," the driver sounded the alert. They saw a small group of people huddled together on the other side of a rise. She asked the driver to stop as she and Sangye exited the taxi and walked over to the people.

"Tashi delek," Tenzin greeted them with her hands pressed together. "I am here for someone," Tenzin said. "A young girl from Nepal. Her name is Yangchen." The group collectively gasped as they couldn't but help mask their surprise hearing Yangchen's name. But they remained quiet. Tenzin went into greater detail of why she was there.

"Forgive for intruding," Tenzin began. "I do not know Yangchen, but I am aware of her quest. And I am here to help, and to make sure you all arrive safely into Lhasa."

The small group of five, three men and two women exchanged glances amongst one another but remained silent. Tenzin sat down next to them, Sangye following. "You see," Tenzin said as she removed her headscarf. "I am here to help. I am the wife of the Supreme Leader, but I am also Tibetan, and all I want is to make sure all of you arrive into Lhasa without any problems or delays."

Still they remained wary. Tenzin thought of another tactic. "Where are you from?" she asked. Again, they remained silent. "Are you from Dharmshala?" she asked. Finally, someone spoke up and said yes.

"Ah, Dharmshala, home of His Holiness," Tenzin acknowledged.

Just then, a Chinese army jeep pulled alongside of them. Tenzin told them to stay quiet. Two soldiers got out of the jeep and pointed their rifles at them. A couple of women started to cry. One of the soldiers shouted to the women and approached them up close, rifles pointed.

"No, no," said one of the women in English. "Don't shoot."

The soldier put his hand out to see their identification. The woman reached into her bag to take it out. Tenzin told her in Tibetan not to show the identification, but she pulled it out in fear of reprisal. She handed it to the soldier. He studied the ID and looked at the woman.

"India?"

He then demanded everyone else's identification as Tenzin and the others refused. He fired his gun into the ground. Everyone then handed them their ID. Tenzin reluctantly handed over hers and stayed quiet. He motioned for Tenzin to stand. The soldier radioed his superior. Tenzin overheard the word *refugees*.

He hung up the radio and approached the small group and asked everyone to stand and put their hands up. This standoff stayed this way for an hour when a helicopter approached the area, with a soft landing that kicked up a cloud of dust. Out came a high official of the army based on his uniform and many badges on both sides of his green army jacket.

He approached the group, as one of the soldiers pointed to Tenzin. He spoke to her in Mandarin, but she answered in English. "I am here to help my people," she said defiantly. The commanding officer grumbled. He walked away and brought out his mobile and made a call. Within a moment, Tenzin could hear he was speaking with someone, and then a pause. He hung up and approached the small group and walked around the circle of people, grumbled a little bit thinking of what to do.

"Stand up," he ordered in English. He then said something in Chinese and the other soldiers took out handcuffs and handcuffed everyone, including Tenzin. Some of the people started to cry, in fear of imprisonment or harm.

CHAPTER THIRTY-TWO

WHEN THE FOUR DEPARTED from their camp, hunger had already set in. Thirst too. This was not the optimal way to be for the next leg of their journey. And finding anyone along the way at night would be almost fruitless at best. They all scraped the bottom of their packs for any crumbs or anything that would give them some nutrition and strength. Although they all appreciated Yangchen's rally talk, running on fumes was affecting them not too long into their latest march. Shigatze wasn't far away as the entire night's walk should get them there, but lack of food and water made the expedition desperate.

Their most dire concern was lack of water. Each person had a few sips remaining in their bottles. Bodhi had looked on the map prior to leaving for any water sources along the way, and the closest one was near Shigatze. They had to cover most of the way with what they had. The hours and pace of their walk were slow. Even though the ground was mostly flat, breathing was labored, and their energy was quickly giving out.

Suddenly, Yangchen collapsed to the ground. The other three rushed around her.

"I feel shaky," she said weakly. "And cold."

Bodhi stood and scanned the dark horizon for any possible movement but was discouraged there wasn't anything. Reaching into his pack for any possible remaining food, he came up empty. Yangchen was flat on the ground. Lobsang let her rest for a few moments then lifted her head and gave her the rest of his water. Chen-tao did too. Bodhi was already out of his water. Things were looking bleak. With no food or water and stranded far away enough from any kind of civilization, a doom unexpectedly consumed the group. They were consigned to the fact that this is where they would stay, as carrying on was impossible at this point. They would wait for daylight, hoping they would spot someone who could save them.

As night gave way to morning, Bodhi stood again to see if he could see anything off in the distance. Nothing and he sat back down. The sun was high in the sky, as the heat bore down. Delirium had set in and he started to walk again towards Shigatze leaving the other three alone with the intent to find help. His pace was slow and laborious placing one foot after the other. Then he collapsed to the ground.

Suddenly, a vehicle approached, dust flying in its wake. The vehicle pulled alongside Bodhi. He lifted his head and saw that it was a Chinese army jeep. Four soldiers jumped out of the jeep with rifles drawn. The soldiers then pointed their rifles straight ahead. Bodhi elevated his head and saw Lobsang and Chen-tao holding up Yangchen walking towards him. Bodhi asked the soldiers for water, but their faces were angry and puzzled. Bodhi made hand movements to indicate the need for water. One of the soldiers finally understood and went to the back of the jeep to get a bottle of water and gave it to Bodhi, who in turn gave it to Yangchen. Lobsang lifted her head to drink it, as she took small sips, then laid back down to rest.

One of the soldiers pointed the rifle at Yangchen indicating that she stands. Lobsang helped her up, as she was wobbly and put his arm around her for support. He then asked them for their identification papers. They were all reluctant to do so, but the soldier barked even louder and clicked his rifle getting ready to fire.

"I think we need to show them," Bodhi said. One by one they handed their ID's and the soldiers' faces turned angry. One of the soldiers radioed someone to get direction. He approached the group of four and ordered them to get into the jeep. When they did, the jeep sped off.

Part Three

Chapter Thirty-Three

THE SCENE WAS TENSE. Tenzin, Sangye and the small group from India continued to stand with rifles pointed towards them, and their hands up in the air. An army jeep approached. Tenzin noticed four non-Army people in the jeep. When it stopped, two soldiers barked for the party to exit the vehicle. As the four were escorted towards Tenzin and her party, her face broke out into a huge smile realizing who they were. She saw a young woman dressed in a very dirty *chuba*. She silently mouthed the name *Yangchen*.

The army officers escorted Yangchen as she could barely stand. Bodhi, Chen-tao, and Lobsang were placed with the group, hands raised. Tenzin rushed up to help Yangchen, wrapped her arms around her. A soldier shouted and pointed his rifle. "She needs help," Tenzin pleaded in Chinese. "And bring water." The soldier made a gesture and stood down and went to huddle with the others on their next course.

Tenzin wanted desperately to speak with Yangchen, but Yangchen was fading as she fell to the ground. "Please!" Tenzin pleaded. "Water."

A bottle of water was brought, and some hard Tibetan bread. Tenzin sat down cradling Yangchen in her lap. She opened the water, lifting Yangchen's head to drink. Yangchen drank some, and Tenzin gave her a bite of bread too. Tenzin maternally and affectionately caressed Yangchen's forehead. Yangchen responded well to the water and bread and started to become responsive. Yangchen looked up at Tenzin, attempting to speak. Her lips and mouth were swollen. Tenzin gave her more water, and another bite of bread.

"Shhh," Tenzin whispered. "I know who you are." Yangchen was confused. One of the soldiers standing next to them barked at Tenzin to remain silent. Yangchen was able to sit on her own now and had become aware. Yangchen saw Bodhi, Lobsang, Chen-tao, Sangye and the people from India standing with their arms still up. Then Bodhi fell to the ground. Yangchen was horrified and stood up. "Hey," she shouted in a hoarse voice to to the soldiers. "Get my friends water and bread, too."

The soldiers saw the desperation but continued to have their rifles drawn. The commander of the army troop ordered food and water to be brought over for everyone, and to lower their arms. The soldiers stood down, water and bread were brought to them. They collectively sat down. Yangchen went to help Bodhi with some water. Everyone else silently drank and ate the bread. The soldier, who was guarding them the closest, moved away to join the other soldiers. Tenzin saw this as her opportunity.

She took out her mobile phone and started to dash off a quick message. The soldier saw Tenzin on her phone and was able to hit send at the last second before he grabbed it out of her hands. The soldier then had everybody turn in their mobile phones and placed them in a plastic bag. They reluctantly complied despite that their batteries had died. The soldier took the phones to his superior, momentarily leaving the prisoners alone. Finally, Tenzin had her opening.

"Yangchen, dear," Tenzin started, "I greatly admire your courage." Yangchen looked at her with confusion and finally spoke.

"But how do you know my name?" she quizzically asked.

"I think all of Tibet and all the Tibetan diaspora will know who you are by the time this is done."

"All I wanted to do was just come to Tibet because of the last wishes from my grandfather," Yangchen said.

"And so, you have," Tenzin said assuredly.

"But we are not in Lhasa and that is my dream, and for my three friends," Yangchen said with a nod to her friends.

"Yangchen," one of the Dharmshala people said, "We are from Dharmshala and found each other on the Tibetan refugee post. We took your advice and came here too."

"Oh!" Yangchen said smiling and surprised. "Tashi delek," she greeted pressing her hands together. "I'm sorry that we are in this mess."

"Don't be sorry, Yangchen," the Dharmshala person said smiling. "Because of you, we are here."

One of the soldiers noticed the lively conversation and came over, pointing his rifle and barked to stay quiet. When everyone finished their water and bread, the soldiers handcuffed them. The sun began to set, as they ordered them to stand and marched them towards Shigatze. When they arrived in town, the soldiers directed them into a nondescript building and had them settle into a small room. The soldiers ordered them to sit, removing the handcuffs, leaving the prisoners alone. Tenzin moved next to Yangchen.

"Yangchen," Tenzin said. "You're probably wondering how I know who you are, and who I am." Yangchen was tired of her long ordeal on the Tibetan Plateau, and simply nodded. Tenzin smiled.

"My name is Tenzin, and I am married to the Chinese Supreme Leader. I am the First Lady of China."

Yangchen gave her a double take of surprise. "But then, why are you here?"

"I am here for you, and everyone in this room," Tenzin said. "To see that you and your friends safely arrive into Lhasa."

Yangchen stayed quiet for a few moments processing what she was just told.

"I see," Yangchen said. "But you are a prisoner like us."

"Yes. I am expecting when my husband discovers I am a prisoner, he will set all of us free." Just then, Bodhi finally joined the conversation.

"Tashi delek, madame," Bodhi said. "I have been the guide for Yangchen and her two friends. It is particularly important we all arrive into Lhasa."

Tenzin nodded pressing her hands to her chest.

"Tashi delek," Tenzin said. "Thank you for escorting Yangchen safely, and her two friends." Bodhi pressed his hands together to his chest in her honor.

"You see, madame, I am Tibetan and American, and I am very familiar with Chinese law and their relationship with Tibet, a very tentative one," Bodhi said. "Do you think they will change the law and allow us to be free?"

"This is my wish," Tenzin said.

Just then, two soldiers flung the door open, and shouted at the prisoners to stay quiet. One of the soldiers threatened them with his rifle, first pointing it towards Yangchen, and then at Tenzin. The soldier turned off the light and all nine people stayed close together as they laid out in the attempt to get some sleep, not knowing their fate.

CHAPTER THIRTY-FOUR

TEMINA'S PHONE VIBRATED, STARTLING her. It was from Tenzin. "*Temina, I am held prisoner in Shigatze by the Chinese army. It is my hope when my husb-*" She gasped as she read it. The son saw Temina's face registering concern.

"Is it mommy?" he asked with worry. Temina looked up and subtly shook her head. She put the children to bed so she could focus on the next step of what to do.

She had the Supreme Leader's mobile number and immediately thought to call him. *But was it the right thing to do?* she wondered. Temina was surely aware of the marriage difficulties between their employers, which made her extremely uncomfortable. However, she remained loyal to Tenzin, and decided not to call the Supreme Leader.

Although Temina was born and raised in Lhasa, she knew few people. But the one person she knew was a friend of hers, Shanti, who was associated with one of the High Lamas at the Potala Palace. She knew Shanti lived in the same home, and despite curfew, took a chance leaving the kids alone to sleep, knowing she would not be gone long.

Temina left the hotel and walked about a kilometer to her friend's house, dashing between streets and alleys, and knocked on the door. It took a few moments, but her friend answered. Shanti was so surprised to see Temina standing there. She invited Temina to enter, as she brought butter tea as they sat drink and had the tea. Temina told her the story of the failing marriage, and Tenzin's attempt to safely see through the refugees' pilgrimage to Lhasa. But in doing so, Tenzin and the refugees were being held prisoner in Shigatze. Shanti sat spellbound listening to Temina's story, tears ran down Temina's troubled face.

"Can you please help me with the High Lama at the Potala?" Temina pleaded.

"Yes, come here tomorrow morning, early, and we shall visit him," Shanti assured her. They exchanged mobile numbers for quick communication.

Temina said goodnight, quickly and safely walked back to the hotel. She checked on the children, who were fast asleep. She felt relieved with the possible solution but spent a sleepless night as she anxiously awaited morning.

***

The children woke Temina up, as it took most of the night to find a couple hours of sleep. Temina bolted out of bed to check her phone. There was a message from her friend to meet with the High Lama as soon as possible at the Potala. She messaged her friend that they would be there soon. "Come, let's get dressed as today we are going on a big adventure to visit the Potala Palace," Temina told the children.

Temina and the children left the hotel and walked to her friend's house, then they took a taxi to the Potala. Her friend saw the High Lama standing outside, waiting for them. Introductions were made as Temina briefly explained the situation. The High Lama saw the possibility that this could lead to a disastrous confrontation, like the 2008 uprising, or worse. Even he was perplexed by the situation and called one of the young monks to summon other High Lamas for consultation. It was only a few minutes later when five High Lamas joined the conversation. Tea was also served. When it was fully explained of the situation out at Shigatze, it was concluded to not communicate with the Supreme Leader; they themselves would go to Shigatze to negotiate with the Chinese army officials.

"We would like you and Shanti to come with us," the High Lama told Temina. "The children may stay here at the Potala. The young monks will look after them."

"Yes, I would like to come," Temina said. "My employer Tenzin needs me. Thank you." Temina explained to the children what their new situation was, and that they would have fun in the palace. She told them this was the home of Kundun before he fled to India. She also told them that the young monk boys would take care of them. They were happy for their own little adventure.

***

After a long day's drive, the minibus reached Shigatze. Six Lamas, Temina and Shanti all piled out. A couple of soldiers had their rifles ready, despite the appearance of the non-threatening group.

The High Lama asked to see the commanding officer of this outfit. The Lama explained that without a release of his prisoners, there would be unrest of the likes Tibet had not seen in twelve years. The commanding officer viewed this as a harmless threat. He told the Lama that the people who crossed were refugees and had been banned from Tibet since 1959.

"This is modern age," explained the High Lama, "And new thinking should be put in place. To have compassion and mercy."

During their heated discussion, the communications officer approached the commanding officer and asked that he be taken aside, away from the discussion.

"What is it?" the commanding officer asked.

"There are two groups from Bhutan and Sikkim that have been taken prisoner near Gyantse." The commanding officer put his hand to his chin, deep in thought of his next move. He went back to the meeting with the High Lamas.

He told them about the latest situation with the other refugee groups. The commanding officer asked the monks to follow him to the room where Tenzin, Yangchen and everyone else were being held. The officer asked the prisoners to stand and come outside. That was a relief to everyone in the room as there was minimal fresh air, just one small barred window. But the commanding officer had them handcuffed again. Tenzin was the last to leave the room.

The Highest Lama, an educated and aware man, recognized Tenzin. He kept quiet about her identity for the moment. The commanding officer told the prisoners that other refugee groups had crossed over to Tibet, from Bhutan and Sikkim. Yangchen broke into a wide smile.

"The others! They're coming!" she said shrieking with glee.

The commanding officer approached Yangchen and stood in front of her for more than a minute before he spoke. Yangchen stood her ground.

"You knew about the others?" he asked gruffly. Yangchen stayed quiet while looking over to Tenzin. Tenzin blinked with a smile. While the soldiers were distracted with their own discussion of what to do about the latest developments, the High Lama approached Tenzin.

"Tashi delek, madame First Lady," the High Lama greeted Tenzin as he pressed his hands to his chest. She replied the same.

"Do you think these soldiers know who you are?" he asked. She shook her head in a no.

"I think we should tell them," he said.

"I liked the secrecy, but I also think you are right," Tenzin said. "Otherwise, this may turn for the worse." She thought for a minute further.

"Yes," she said. "My husband should finally know I am here with the refugees."

The commanding officer and other soldiers approached the group of Lamas and prisoners.

"We are going to take you, to..." the commanding officer started but the High Lama interrupted him.

"There is something you should know," the High Lama said. Just then, Tenzin stepped forward.

"I am the First Lady," Tenzin said. The soldiers gaped at her, and instantly recognized her now. The soldiers were speechless for a moment.

"But why are you here?" the officer asked.

"To help my fellow Tibetans," she said defiantly. "That is why. And I suggest you relay my husband of this situation. And please remove our handcuffs," as she defiantly thrusted her handcuffed hands into the air.

The soldiers retreated to discuss everything. The commanding officer placed a call. Tenzin tried to listen, but he was far enough away that Tenzin could not hear except for the words *First Lady*. She took some delight wondering how her husband would react to this news, and at the minimum, he would certainly be wondering the fate of his children. Tenzin was optimistic.

Yangchen approached the High Lama.

"Excuse me, High Lama," Yangchen said as she pressed her hands to her chest. "I am Yangchen. I would like to ask you if you know Panchen High Lama Gyatso." The High Lama looked at her with surprise and smiled.

"Yes, I remember him, of course," he said. "We were like brothers." Yangchen beamed.

"You are Panchen High Lama Kelsang?"

"Yes, my child." Yangchen became visibly excited.

"He was my grandfather," she said, smiling and then turning sad. "But he passed away last year."

The High Lama called the other Lamas over.

"Come. Meet the granddaughter of Panchen High Lama Gyatso," said the High Lama. They all bowed, pressing their hands together and started a chant in honor of Yangchen's grandfather. The commanding officer was distracted by this and told the Lamas to stay quiet, while interrupting their prayer.

"Ignore them," the High Lama said. "It is an honor to meet you, Yangchen."

Yangchen bowed deeply in honor and respect for the High Lamas.

The commanding officer came back and told the prisoners they would be taken to a holding area just outside Lhasa. They were to rendezvous with the other two groups from Sikkim and Bhutan.

Tenzin approached Yangchen. "Now you will have your wish, to go to Lhasa," Tenzin said. "My husband will free us so you will finally be in the center of your homeland."

CHAPTER THIRTY-FIVE

LI WAS WOKEN IN the middle of the night out of an agitated sleep with a gentle knock on the door by his trusted aid and confidant.

"Yes?" His aid entered the room.

"My Supreme Leader," he said nervously. Li turned on his bedside lamp. The aid rushed to his bed and stood in front of him. Li squirmed to sit upright. His aid hesitated to speak.

"Go on," Li said firmly.

"There is news from Lhasa," he said hesitantly. Li looked at him, giving him the space to speak. "Refugees from Nepal, India, Bhutan and Sikkim have crossed into Tibet." Li stayed silent as he knew this based on the text message Tenzin had received. "They are being held prisoner in Shigatze."

"There is more news," the aid said. "Your wife, the First Lady. She is also held prisoner and is now being transported to Lhasa."

"What about my children?" Li asked.

"I don't know," the aid reluctantly said.

Li jumped out of bed. He had been distraught that his wife had left and taken their children along. Yet his duties prevented him from leaving Beijing. Now he had to go. Li thought for a moment.

"Arrange my plane to Lhasa, quickly." The aid left the room while Li prepared for his trip.

CHAPTER THIRTY-SIX

A CONVOY OF ARMY jeeps and the minibus departed from Shigatze for Gyantse to pick up the other refugees and on to Lhasa. The minibus carried Tenzin, Yangchen, Lobsang, Bodhi and Chen-tao, as well as the people from Dharmshala. They had spent a restless night and still were unsure of what was to happen except for the simple fact that they were at least making their way towards Lhasa. The driver and a rifle-carrying soldier were in the front seat. Tenzin made sure she sat next to Yangchen. She put her arm around Yangchen as she felt so motherly and close to her. They tried to speak but the soldier squelched any conversation. It was crowded in the minibus, and it would take the better part of the day to arrive into Gyantse.

After an uneventful trip, they arrived. The lead convoy jeep pulled alongside an old, dilapidated building. The minibus passengers were told to wait. Tenzin asked that they get out and stretch. The soldier allowed and escorted them inside the building for a bite to eat and refresh. There were momos waiting for them, and Tenzin thought that because of her First Lady status, they all got some extra care.

Tenzin and Yangchen were alone in the restroom. Tenzin came close to Yangchen's ear.

"My dear Yangchen," Tenzin began. "You must be proud that you started a movement. A movement we people of Tibet have wanted for sixty years." Yangchen smiled.

"But it was so simple. My parents gave me a smartphone for my eighteenth birthday," Yangchen told Tenzin. "It started with my post online...but I didn't think it could really happen. I mean everybody who has come."

The soldier standing guard outside told them to stay quiet. Yangchen crinkled up her nose to the soldier. Tenzin poopooed him waving her hand. Yangchen leaned onto her.

"Do you think your husband will really set us free?" Yangchen asked. Tenzin whispered to Yangchen.

"Let me explain," Tenzin started. "When we first were to be married, I told him I would marry him if he would help my people, all of Tibet and its refugees." Tenzin was quiet in order not to be reprimanded again for talking by the soldier. She continued.

"This will be his test to do what is right for his family, not just for Tibet."

When Tenzin, Yangchen and the group reconvened outside under the watchful eyes of the soldiers, the others from Sikkim and Bhutan joined the group. One of the members from that group asked if Yangchen was here.

"Yes, I am Yangchen," she said, identifying herself. The people from Sikkim and Bhutan bowed and prayed in Yangchen's honor. "I am happy you were successful in your crossing."

The commanding officer overheard this conversation and approached Yangchen.

"As I suspected," he said firmly. "You are the responsible one for this movement." Yangchen stayed quiet.

"You will ride with me in the jeep," he bellowed.

A second minibus was waiting to carry the Sikkim and Bhutan people, as everyone except Yangchen piled into their respective vehicles for the five-hour drive to Lhasa.

***

Li had arrived into Lhasa prior to the convoy. Upon landing, he was told that the convoy from Gyantse was on its way to Lhasa. Li was also told that his children were at the Potala Palace. He asked to be taken straight away. When he arrived surrounded by guards, he rushed to see them. They were outside playing football with some young monk boys. When they saw their father, they ran to him as he lifted both the children up in his arms and kissed them both enthusiastically.

"Where is your mother?" Li asked.

"She is with Temina," the boy said.

"I see," he said.

"And your mother dropped you here at the Potala?"

"No," the boy said. "Temina did."

Li was surprised that his wife would be so bold in her actions, as well as Temina. He knew she loved their children and assumed leaving them at the Potala was a safe place. And he also knew that above all, other than their children, taking care of Tibetan people and their situations was a priority for her. This resonated in his head.

"I have good news," Li told them. "Your mother is coming back to Lhasa. We will stay tonight, and, in the morning, we will go see her. Okay?"

"Okay," the kids squirmed away to play more football with the monk boys.

Li's close aid and confidant had accompanied him to Lhasa and was very aware of the situation. He approached Li.

"What are you going to do, my Supreme Leader?" the aid asked. "Will you release the refugees and the First Lady?"

CHAPTER THIRTY-SEVEN

YANGCHEN RODE UP FRONT with the commanding officer. He asked her many questions, which normally would be a tiresome task, but Yangchen proudly stood her ground.

"How did you arrange this crossing of refugees from many countries?" he asked.

"From my phone, sir," Yangchen said proudly. "With a phone you can do everything, even organize a movement." She giggled at her own remark. The commanding officer simply gruffed.

As the jeep drove on, Yangchen became excited to see Lhasa for the first time. But she was also concerned she would only see a prison cell.

"Will you set us free in Lhasa, sir?" she asked.

"No, we are taking you to prison," he said. "You have violated Chinese law." Yangchen crinkled her nose at his statement.

"But sir," she started. "All we mean to do is return to our homeland, nothing more."

"That does not matter," he said firmly. "Law is law."

"Phooey on your law, sir," Yangchen said defiantly. "Imagine. You are from China, and you are a prisoner in Japan. Wouldn't you want more than anything in the world to return to China?"

The commanding officer stayed quiet and gave what she said some thought.

"You are a brave girl, Yangchen," he said. "There will be discussions on what to do with you and your refugees."

"What about Tenzin, the First Lady?" she asked.

"The Supreme Leader will manage that situation."

* * *

Tenzin's minibus rode behind the jeep in which Yangchen was traveling. Conversation was minimal. She wondered how her children were doing. She also knew that her husband was most likely waiting for her. She hoped for the best; for her, for Yangchen and everyone. But she wasn't confident, despite being the mother of their children. 'Law is law' he would always say when she brought up the subject to free Tibetan people. *What was he afraid of by changing the law?* she wondered.

Bodhi, who sat behind Tenzin, tapped her on the shoulder and whispered into her ear.

"Madame First Lady," he started. "I happen to know that the Chinese people love Tibet. They even built a train to take people there. I think Chinese people would support a free Tibet."

"I believe you are right, Mr. Bodhi," she said. "But I am not sure about the Supreme Leader."

"I am certain of it," he said. "It is time for change, and our mutual friend Yangchen started it. God bless her."

"Yes, God bless her," Tenzin said.

The sun began to set in the sky and cast its rays on the Potala Palace. The convoy was about to enter the outskirts of Lhasa.

CHAPTER THIRTY-EIGHT

THE STATELY AND HISTORIC Potala Palace was now in plain sight. Yangchen marveled at how proudly it stood on top of the highest peak in Lhasa proper as the convoy entered the outskirts of the city. But instead of heading straight towards the palace, the commanding officer turned on a dirt road where nothing was around.

There were local Tibetan people walking past the entrance to the compound who were unnerved and curious what the convoy was all about. They stopped in their tracks to observe. It was a short distance from the main gate to where the convoy pulled into the military prison compound area. Chinese army guards were everywhere with much comings and goings of the rifle-carrying soldiers. A group of about twenty soldiers waited for the convoy to stop their vehicles. They drew their rifles.

The commanding officer exited his jeep, telling Yangchen to stay put. He approached the lead soldier of the group of twenty. Yangchen saw them converse as she sat alone in the jeep pondering her fate. She was resigned to the fact of imprisonment but also had faith it would be temporary. She thought of her family back in Nepal and realized they must be panicking about her status and condition.

Tenzin anxiously awaited meeting her husband, and ultimately what he would do. Finally, the refugees were asked to leave the vehicles. They were handcuffed again and led single file into the prison compound, the soldiers' rifles drawn all the while. The local Tibetan people saw the prisoners and wondered what was going on. One of the Tibetans approached the guards at the front and inquired about the convoy. The guards ignored them. One person discreetly took a picture with his phone of the group.

One of the soldiers counted all the refugees. He told the commanding officer there were sixteen in total from the three countries, Sikkim being part of India along with the others from Dharmshala. There were four from Bhutan and Yangchen's party. Plus, the First Lady for a total of seventeen. The soldier asked if the First Lady would be a prisoner.

"Yes, until the Supreme Leader says otherwise."

They were led inside the prison entrance. All were nervous and, for the time, disappointed to come as far as Lhasa and not be able to see it.

"Don't worry, my friends," Yangchen said assuredly. "We will see Lhasa."

The refugees were asked to wear prison clothes and to hand over their clothes when they had changed. And then finally, the women were led to one prison cell, and the men to the other cell.

Yangchen and Tenzin, along with the other people sat on hard-wooden benches, settling into their new and stark surroundings in the dark and cold cell.

"What do we do?" Yangchen asked Tenzin.

"We wait," Tenzin responded.

"I hope they can release us soon," Yangchen said.

"Me too," Tenzin replied. "Me too."

But nothing happened. They were given meager food of stale momos. Yangchen nervously paced around the small cell. All she wanted was to be released so she could finally see the fabled city without any encumbrances of imprisonment. Still, nothing happened. It was now night. Tenzin assumed her husband was in Lhasa and was surprised he hadn't made an appearance yet.

There were enough benches to lie down on, and that is what they did for the night.

* * *

Meanwhile, the Tibetan local, who had taken a picture of the refugees with his phone, posted it on a local social media site. The man asked if anyone knew who the mysterious prisoners were that accompanied the picture. Although the picture of the prisoners was taken from a distance, it clearly showed Yangchen, Tenzin, and the others dressed in *chubas* or Buddhist orange and yellow robes. Within minutes, the post went viral.

Someone on the post suggested they go to the entrance of the military prison and find out what they could do. The next day, a crowd gathered outside the entrance of the military prison. First, it was ten people, but as the day wore on, there were hundreds, sitting quietly and respectfully in order not to become prisoners themselves. The army soldiers asked them to leave, but they did not. They sat down in their places, chanting prayers, and twirling prayer wheels.

Just then, a convoy of stately cars converged upon the prison entrance and turned into the military compound. The photographer, who had since become the proxy leader, stood to walk across the road to get a better glimpse of who this could be. The guards at the entrance drew their rifles to keep him at bay. But before they moved back across the street, some of the people saw the doors to the vehicles open, and from a distance they could see it was the Supreme Leader of all of China.

Chapter Thirty-Nine

LI ENTERED THE PRISON and was escorted to a meeting area. Tenzin was told she had a visitor, and knew it was her husband.

"Please tell the visitor to come see me at my cell," Tenzin demanded. The guard hesitated. "I want him to see my friends, how harmless they are, and how they should not be treated this way." The guard left. It wasn't long before Li entered the prison cell area and saw Tenzin and the other women sitting in their cell. Tenzin stood up from the bench and approached her husband at the bars. They stood face to face. The tension was thick.

"I will have you released," Li told her coldly.

"No," Tenzin said. "Not until you free everybody here."

"I cannot do that," Li said reprimanding her.

"Then do not release me," she said firmly. "Not until everyone can go."

Li stood his ground. Bodhi, who was just next to the women's cell, stood to listen.

"Excuse me, sir," Bodhi said. "You are acting in old China thinking. Everyone from all over the world, including China care about Tibet and its people. People will be happy if you free Tibet, and you will go down in history as the Supreme Leader with passion for Tibet."

Li gave Bodhi an up and down look but didn't say anything. Then he turned around and left the cell area without saying goodbye to his wife.

"Sir, if you love your family, you will know what to do," Yangchen shouted at Li.

He stopped and stood straight, then half turned around and looked at Yangchen.

"And who are you?" he asked tersely.

"I'm Yangchen, sir," she said proudly. "I'm the one you can hold responsible for this."

Li looked at her with boiling consternation, then walked out. Everyone was stunned. The silence was deafening. Tenzin began to cry. Yangchen approached her.

"You are a strong lady, also like Joan of Arc," she said. Tenzin smiled.

"So are you, dearest Yangchen, so are you." They gave each other a strong, loving embrace, parted, and went to sit back down not knowing how long this vigil was to last.

Yangchen went around the prison cell asking each person why they took the dangerous journey to Lhasa. Everyone's answers were the same. Their families crossed from Tibet to India, or Nepal, or Bhutan or Sikkim to escape the brutal regime in 1959 and the subsequent years. They explained their family's history that once the news spread that the Dalai Lama had made it safely to India, they and thousands of others crossed to the various neighboring countries and became Tibetan refugees. From generation to generation, just as Yangchen's grandfather had done. It was comforting for Yangchen to hear their stories firsthand, all like-minded with similar situations. But Yangchen's mood shifted and soured.

"If the Chinese leader wouldn't release Tenzin, why would they release us?" Yangchen asked. Yangchen could see the deep concern on Tenzin's face. She instantly regretted saying that. She moved next to Tenzin.

"Don't worry, Tenzin," she sympathized. "I feel the karma; he will do what is right for you and your family."

"We have two children," Tenzin said, tears running down her face. "And I miss them, and they will not understand why I am not with them. I feel awful."

"That is why I believe he will take care of this," Yangchen said. "I am sure of it."

***

Li went to retrieve his two children at the Potala and was staged at the airport, waiting for their flight back to Beijing. Upon boarding and settling in their seats, the children started crying.

"Where is mommy?" they asked. "Why isn't she coming home?"

He didn't know what to say. While he tried to console them, there was nothing he could do to stop their crying. Except for one thing. Li jumped out of his seat and shouted, "Open the door, we're going back to Lhasa."

CHAPTER FORTY

BY NOW, THE CROWD outside the prison had grown to thousands of people in support of the prisoners. The army kept a tight lid as to who the prisoners were. The crowd knew from history, those who were held as prisoners went against the laws of the Chinese government. The consequences of such action were incredibly dangerous. There were constant chants and drum beating, prayer wheel twirling, and high lamas all in unison to support the prisoners. Till now, the army let the people be.

The supreme leader took his children by the hand to head back to the prison. "Now we're going to see your mother." They were excited. Li was informed of the crowd outside the gate and ordered for the crowd to be dispersed. But the crowd stayed firm and continued to sit, despite the semi-forceful ways of the soldiers literally dragging the people up on their feet. They sat back down as soon as they stood. The soldiers felt it was useless and radioed to advise command of the strongminded situation and awaited the next level of command on what to do.

***

Yangchen, Tenzin and the other women as well as the men heard the chants of the protesters. They felt a sense of calm for the support of those outside the prison. They themselves started to chant.

"Chant loudly and let them hear us!" Yangchen boldly shouted. Both the men and women chanted loudly. Those outside picked up on the chant inside the prison. The proxy leader stood to quieten the crowd down in order to listen to the prisoners. The chant ended, and for a moment, it was quiet. Then the protesters erupted with a yell and shout of support. The prisoners heard this too, and then shouted back.

The back and forth chanting went on for a while. Just then, a convoy of black cars turned into the prison. The crowd stood to observe what was to happen next. They saw the Supreme Leader exit one of the cars. Then they started to boo and hiss.

"I had ordered to disperse the crowd," Li barked at the Commander.

"They will not obey, Supreme Leader," the Commander responded.

"Never mind," Li said angrily. "Take me inside."

Li entered the prison and asked that his children stay in the car. He did not want them to see their mom in prison. He was escorted back to the cell where Tenzin was. When she saw him, she remained quiet and steadfast. If he didn't release everyone, she was determined to sustain this vigil. He approached the cell and came face to face with Tenzin. She held on to the cell bars, for defiance, for control.

"Tenzin, I would like to speak with you," Li said.

"Anything you have to say, you can say to me here," she said defiantly. Li looked down, lost in momentary thought. Then he let out a big exhale and muttered, "Okay," as if he had finally convinced himself.

"I will change the rule," he said quietly. "Your friends can go free." Tenzin's face brightened as did everyone's within earshot. "And we're going home."

"Really?" Yangchen shouted. "Are you for real?"

"Yes, Miss Yangchen," Li said. "Your heroics were actually inspiring. Tibetan refugees owe you much."

"You mean to say everyone can come?" she asked. "From Nepal, India and everywhere?"

Li nodded his head to say yes.

"Yes!" she shouted. "Thank you, sir." Yangchen bowed and pressed her hands to her chest.

"Excuse me, sir," Bodhi jumped in. "When exactly may we go free?"

"Now," Li said shouting, "Guards. Unlock these doors."

The guards unlocked both doors and the former prisoners were directed to register their names and nationalities. Yangchen was first to fill out a brief form and put Tibet as her nationality. Despite her love and appreciation for Nepal, Tibet was her homeland. One by one, the others filled out the form as well. Li took Tenzin aside.

"Are you happy now, dear?"

"Yes. Thank you," Tenzin said. But she was also a bit sad. "I don't want to go back to Beijing right now. I want to see my friends enjoy their time in Lhasa."

"That is fine," he said. "We can stay here for a while."

With all the paperwork finished, they were told they were free to go.

"Hey, wait a minute," Yangchen said. "We want our phones and our packs."

In a corner in a pile were their packs. The original commanding officer held the bag with their phones and laid them out on a table for the owners to claim them. Yangchen took hers, also removing the charger from her pack, looked for a plug, and found one. She sat on the floor to get a little bit of battery charge. Everyone else was ready to leave and asked her to come.

"Five minutes," she said. "I have something important to do." She asked one of the prison administrators if they had Wi-Fi. The administrator said yes as there was enough juice on her phone to find the Wi-Fi link. She went back to her original post on the Tibetan refugee site and posted the following:

'I am in Lhasa. And we are free! Now everyone can come.'

She also wrote to her family that she was safe in Lhasa. Before she could unplug her charger, Yangchen received her family's reply.

'We are so proud of you, brave Yangchen!'

Yangchen smiled broadly and was so proud and pleased, and relieved. She breathed a sigh and hoisted her pack on her back and firmly held her phone in her hand.

"OK, I am ready to leave," she said.

Tenzin told Li she would walk the remaining way to the center of Lhasa with Yangchen and her friends. As they left the police station, her children patiently waiting in the car, opened the door and ran to their mother. She picked them both up and hugged and kissed and everyone cried.

"Let's all walk to Lhasa," Yangchen excitedly said.

CHAPTER FORTY-ONE

YANGCHEN LED THE PROCESSION single file outside the prison gates. The large crowd that had gathered stood, silently bowed, and prayed out of respect and honor. The man who had taken the picture and was the proxy leader of the protesters, approached Yangchen.

"Who are you people?" he asked.

"We were refugees," she said. "But no more. Today, we are Tibetans."

"What do you mean, refugees?" he asked.

"We came from Nepal, India, and Bhutan. Our families are from Tibet."

"You crossed over the Himalayas?" he asked in shock.

"Yes," Yangchen calmly answered.

"Om manne padme hum," the man reverently recited, while placing his hands together to chest and bowed.

The man looked at Yangchen again and then down the line of the rest of the refugees. The crowd was dead silent to hear what Yangchen had to say. The man delivered Yangchen's message by shouting to the crowd and lifting the mystery of who the prisoners were. A big chorus of cheers rang from the crowd. It was time to move on.

Following Yangchen was Tenzin, Li, and their two children. Then Lobsang, Chen-tao and the others from

India, Bhutan, and Sikkim. Bodhi was last. It was about a two-kilometer walk straight ahead to the Potala, and then another couple of kilometers to the Jokhang Temple and the Barkhor Bazaar. Without ever being here, Yangchen knew Lhasa well from studying so many books and pictures, so she knew where to go.

Following the procession of former prisoners and refugees were the thousands of Tibetan protesters. Cars that would pass by honked their horns. Some of them even parked their cars and motor scooters along the side of the road, jumped out, and joined the massive procession marching towards the center of Lhasa. It was late in the afternoon and a slight chill cooled down the marchers as the sun began to set behind the mountains.

When Yangchen came upon the Potala, she looked up at the thirteen storied high sacred palace regally sitting on top of a hill. The procession stopped behind. Lobsang stood next to her.

"We made it, Yangchen," he said emotionally. She turned to give him a big and long-lasting hug. The crowd cheered. Tenzin approached Yangchen and Lobsang.

"Congratulations, dear," Tenzin said. "Your bravery is now being rewarded. Isn't it magnificent?" Yangchen was in awe. But they weren't finished. What she looked forward to the most, in all her dreams, and all her conversations with her grandfather, was to circumambulate around the Jokhang and into the Barkhor Bazaar.

"Come on," Yangchen said, and she started to walk towards the Jokhang.

With all that they had walked and trekked and climbed since Nepal, this was the easiest part. Yangchen led a slow pace, despite being so excited to arrive. She wanted to savor those steps. Just ahead, she could see people in their clockwise circumambulation around the Jokhang. Yangchen stopped for a moment and removed her backpack from her back and set it on the ground. Everyone behind stopped as well. Whatever Yangchen did, they all followed.

She took out the two wooden blocks, putting her backpack on her back. Bodhi, who was still behind, saw what she was doing and moved up front. "Here, let me carry your backpack."

Yangchen took a block for each hand and got down on her knees and glided her way to a full-body prostration parallel to the ground, went back on her knees, then stood straight up, clapping the two pieces of wood, and repeated these steps over and over. Some of the other Tibetans did the same as it is the most sacred ceremony and celebration of the most sacred place in all of Tibet, and the world. Full body prostration is the deepest kind of ritual any Tibetan can do.

She huffed and puffed with Lhasa's elevation at four thousand meters. It was difficult to focus on what was ahead, but Yangchen could hear the murmurs of the crowd as she circumambulated all the way. When she stood, she saw that they had arrived. Hundreds of people walked slowly, round and round, with prayer wheels or prayer beads while quietly murmuring sacred chants, oblivious to the new throngs of arrivals. She was mesmerized.

Yangchen turned to see that Lobsang was right behind her. And behind Lobsang, Chen-tao and finally Bodhi. The original four. Bodhi came up her side.

"Shall we?" he said boyishly with a big smile.

She nodded her head once and joined in with the ones who were already circumambulating. Yangchen was finally one of them. She kept pace with everyone else while she looked up at the Jokhang and the procession ahead. They turned the corner of the Jokhang. Just behind the sacred temple was the main marketplace in all of Tibet, the Barkhor Bazaar. Yangchen's eyes lit up at the sight of all kinds of things that were available to purchase, everything from yak meat and yak cheese to ancient trinkets, to clothes of course, and electronics as well. It was a cornucopia of everything.

But Yangchen didn't stop. She wanted to keep walking around and planned to do it a few times. All the while, her fellow refugees from Bhutan, Sikkim, India, and the protestors continued to follow in Yangchen's footsteps. The Chinese soldiers guarding the Jokhang area were in shock when they spotted that their Supreme Leader and his family were also part of this extraordinary procession. Some of the soldiers gathered away from their post to discuss the odd situation. Li saw this activity and jumped out of the procession and approached the soldiers. He held his two children in his arms, with Tenzin by his side. He saw the local commanding officer and summoned him over as he placed the children back down. They went to hug at both sides of their mom, so happy she was with them again.

"Today, I have set the people of Tibet free. You may guard as you wish. But convey to all Chinese soldiers of Tibet to let any refugees from other countries cross over, and do not bother them and let them come in peace."

The commanding officer hesitated in trying to understand what was just said by the Supreme Leader and this new governing law. "You do as I say, effective immediately!" he demanded.

The commanding officer saluted and walked away and went to send a message to all throughout Tibet. Tenzin heard every word and came up to her husband and hugged in full view of everyone.

"Thank you, my dear husband," she cooed into his ear. "I am proud of you. Do you remember ten years ago you came to my rescue for my mother? Right here in this square." Li smiled. "Of course, I do," he said sweetly. "This was the right decision," he whispered into her ear.

"You did what was right, for Tibet," she said. "And for your family." She kissed him on the cheek.

Yangchen had stopped and observed the reunion of her friend Tenzin and her husband. She smiled and pressed her hands to her chest. Out of the corner of her eyes, Tenzin saw Yangchen and bowed the same. The family went over to see Yangchen.

"You are a brave young lady," Li told her. "All of Tibet will forever be in your compassion and your courage will be admired throughout the world."

"Thank you, sir," Yangchen said humbly. Tenzin moved in front of Yangchen, face to face.

"I found a true friend on this journey," Tenzin said. She bowed as Yangchen did the same. "As did I," Yangchen said. The two became teary-eyed and hugged.

"We shall have you for dinner before we leave back to Beijing," Tenzin said. "Where will you be?"

"Right here," Yangchen said with glowing happiness. "Hang on a moment. Let's take a selfie."

She pulled up the camera on her phone. She must have been in range of free Wi-Fi, as she saw there were hundreds of notifications from her Tibet refugee online post. She gasped as she started to read some of them.

Bodhi, Lobsang, Chen-tao and Tenzin all stood nearby, rushed up to her crowding around.

"Good news?" Bodhi asked. Yangchen was completely distracted and put her hand to her mouth in shock and amazement.

"Yangchen?" Bodhi said. "What is it?" She looked at him and everyone. Her mouth half open and in shock, and then she burst out in tears.

"What is it, Yangchen, dear?" Tenzin asked.

"They're coming," she said, tears streaming down her face. "Everyone. They're coming. Everyone is coming...We did it!" She showed them her phone as they crowded around to read some of the messages that all said: *We are coming too.*

This was the moment when Yangchen realized she had started a movement on the unimaginable grandest of scales.

***

The celebration lasted through the night. It was a nonstop flow of circumambulating, resting, eating as some locals would hand them rice bowls and momos... and more walking. All those who joined her from the beginning, even the protesters, stayed with her. She had become a hero to all of Tibet.

Yangchen said she wanted to see the sunrise while listening to the monks' early morning chant at nearby Sera and Drepung monasteries that her grandfather had told her so much about.

"Listen," Yangchen said. The distinctive deep baritone resonating chants could be heard, she knew her journey was complete. She cried. She cried for such joy.

"I made it, grandfather," she said tenderly. "I made it."

Bodhi came up to her and paternally put his arm around her shoulder. "You did good, Yangchen. You and Joan of Arc are now linked in history."

"Yes, I guess so," she said wiping away her tears.

"I'm going to see my mom now, and bring her this medication," he declared. "I'll see you around."

Yangchen gave him a big hug. "Thank you, Bodhi," she cooed. "Thank you."

Chen-tao came up to Yangchen.

"My monk brothers back home will honor you forever," he said while bowing, hands together.

"But Chen-tao," she said reverently. "We are home." He smiled and moved out of circumambulation and went ahead to see his father who had been held in prison for years.

Yangchen wasn't sure what she was going to do next, but she wasn't all that concerned about it. She was finally here, living her's and her grandfather's dream. Lobsang and Yangchen sat face to face with each other. She yawned. Lobsang smiled. "Suddenly I'm so sleepy," she said. "Me too," Lobsang said. "A long day."

"I think I'll just lay down a while and rest, Lobsang." Yangchen took out a towel she had carried with her since Nepal and spread the towel out to lay down in the shadow of the Jokhang Temple, in the center in all of Tibet. Despite the chill of the cool, spring morning air, the dutiful Lobsang sat by Yangchen as she fell fast asleep listening to the monks' sacred chants.

~The End~

www.ingramcontent.com/pod-product-compliance
Ingram Content Group UK Ltd.
Pitfield, Milton Keynes, MK11 3LW, UK
UKHW041955190726
13854UKWH00005B/1986

9 789389 932461